'You don't l
alone. Let me

Tears stung her e
away, not wanting   them. He drew
her close, wrapping his arms around her. His
closeness, the intimacy of having his strong
arms hold her, shattered her fragile defences.
She drank in the warmth and comfort of his
embrace like a flower that had gone without
water for too long. His shoulder was there for
her and the temptation was too great to resist.
As his hand curved around the back of her
head and tangled with the silk of her hair, she
leaned her cheek against his chest for a
moment, absorbing the shelter he offered.

A&E DRAMA

Blood pressure is high and pulses are racing in these fast-paced dramatic stories from Mills & Boon® Medical Romance™. They'll move a mountain to save a life in an emergency, be they the crash team, emergency doctors, or paramedics. There are lots of critical engagements amongst the high tensions and emotional passions in these exciting stories of lives and loves at risk!

Recent titles by Joanna Neil:

IN HIS
TENDER CARE

BY
JOANNA NEIL

MILLS & BOON®

*First published in Great Britain 2005
Harlequin Mills & Boon Limited,
Eton House, 18-24 Paradise Road, Richmond, Surrey TW9 1SR*

© Joanna Neil 2005

ISBN 0 263 84325 4

*Set in Times Roman 10½ on 12½ pt.
03-0805-45111*

*Printed and bound in Spain
by Litografia Rosés, S.A., Barcelona*

CHAPTER ONE

'CASEY... Casey, please, stop.' The childish voice
floated across the air and Sasha frowned a little as she
slowed her car on a bend in the road. The window
was wound down because even this early in the morning, not much past breakfast-time, the sun was strong,
and she wanted to enjoy its warm touch on her arm.
It meant that she could hear everything quite clearly,
and it struck her that there was a note of urgency in
that cry. What was going on?

'It isn't safe. Please, Casey, come away from
there.' The girl was pleading now.

Sasha slowed the car to a crawl and glanced
obliquely towards the child. Luckily, there wasn't too
much traffic on the road, and she paused to take in
her surroundings. She wasn't used to this area in
Wales and she was still finding her way around,
though she had discovered that this was the most
pleasant route to the hospital where she was going to
be working.

For the most part of this journey, she had been
driving along country lanes, and it was only now, as
she approached the outskirts of the town, that things
were beginning to change. Right now, she was pass-
ing by what looked like an old factory unit that was
in varying stages of demolition.

Wire fencing surrounded the site, but Sasha saw a small child, a girl of about eight years old standing by the fence, an anxious expression on her face as she looked towards the partly bulldozed building. Inside the fenced area, Sasha caught a faint movement, and then glimpsed the figure of a young boy, gingerly climbing one of the crumbling walls.

Shocked, she drew the car to a halt alongside the pavement and watched as the boy swung himself up onto a half-landing, which was partially supported by the remnants of some stairs. Then, as Sasha held her breath, he began to tread cautiously across what had once been a section of floor.

Worried now, Sasha clambered out of the car. She had to do something…she had to try to stop him before he hurt himself. Before she could reach the fencing, though, she knew that she was already too late. The section of floor he was standing on began to give way and in the next moment the boy was falling, his body angled towards a twisted metal support.

Sasha's heart was thumping hard, pounding in her throat. There was no way she could reach him in time, and his shout of pain as he hit the metal strut tore at her, dragging a gasp of air from her lungs. Then there was no sound at all. He lay still, his body crumpled like a rag doll.

Sasha was running now. The little girl had started to cry, heavy, anguished sobs, and as she reached her, Sasha asked quickly, 'How did he get in there, do you know?'

The child was frightened, tears staining her cheeks.

'He climbed over,' she answered shakily. 'I told him not to do it, but he didn't listen to me.' She pointed to where the fencing was bent out of shape. Part of it had been cut away, and Sasha guessed that some of the local youths must have been at work, trying to find a way in. 'He's my brother. I told him we shouldn't go in there.'

'I'll try to get to him,' Sasha said. 'I'll do what I can to help him.' She reached in her jacket pocket and handed her mobile phone to the girl. 'Do you know how to use this?' When the child nodded, Sasha breathed a sigh of relief. 'Good girl. I'm going to get some things from my car. Call the emergency service, and ask for an ambulance. Tell the operator what has happened, and where we are.'

The child dashed away her tears and began to press buttons. Sasha hurried back to her car and pulled open the boot, grabbing her emergency medical bag. Then she studied the fence for a moment, looking for the best footholds. It wasn't going to be easy, especially with her bag to hinder her, but she didn't see what else she could do. From the look of him, the boy was badly injured, and she needed to get to him fast.

Winding the strap of her bag over her shoulders, she heaved herself up, testing the fence for handholds, and then she scrambled up as best she could. Once over the top, she jumped down and looked around, trying to judge the best way of getting to him. She would have to climb over the rubble and wreckage of the building to reach him.

The ground beneath her feet was unstable, and at

one point she slipped and gashed her ankle on some brickwork. Gritting her teeth, she went on, thankful there were no further mishaps to hinder her before she reached him at last. Climbing up to him, she gripped an overhead joist that appeared stable, and released a shower of brick dust onto her head. Brushing the worst of it off with her hand, she steadied herself on a heap of shattered masonry, and then studied the child briefly.

He was about ten years old, she guessed. He was hunched over the strut, and as she looked at him she could see that his eyes were open, but it was clear that he was in shock and scarcely able to respond.

She spoke softly to him. 'Casey, I'm a doctor. I'm going to do what I can to help you. All right?'

He mumbled something incoherent, and she checked his pulse. It was fast, and his breathing was shallow and rapid. Blood seeped from a wound in his abdomen.

She gently stroked his face in a comforting gesture. She would have to move him, but doing that could cause massive haemorrhaging. She winced, debating the best way of going about it.

'Sweetheart, I'm going to have to lift you off this support and I need you to work with me on this, and trust me.'

'Don't try to move him.' A voice sounded behind her, clipped, authoritative, deeply masculine, and it shook her rigid, coming out of nowhere like that. While she gathered her breath, the voice went on sharply, 'You could cause a lot of damage when you don't know what you're doing. You should always wait for expert back-up.'

She half turned, and stared at the man. How had he managed to get here without her knowing about it? She had been concentrating on getting to the boy, and she had heard nothing, but now the man was standing here, large as life, his immaculately shod feet braced on the stonework. He wasn't having any trouble keeping his balance on the rugged, uneven ground.

He was tall and lean, grey-suited, his jacket open to reveal a perfectly laundered linen shirt beneath it. He was in his mid-thirties, she surmised, and his features were sculpted, his hair crisp and black as jet.

Frowning, she said in a winded tone, 'You gave me the shock of my life, creeping up on me like that. How did you get here?' Was he a passer-by who had followed her, or was he the man in charge of the site—or someone from the company that was going to build here? No wonder he had followed her so swiftly. Did he have a key to the gate? She started to try to ease the bag off her back, but it was awkward while she was trying to keep her footing on uneven ground and she was in danger of toppling over.

It was awful to think that something like this could happen to a small child when better preventative measures could have been taken. Without giving the man time to answer, she went on sharply, 'I hope you're not responsible for this building site. With children around you need more of a deterrent than a plain wire fence.'

He simply gazed at her in disbelief, and she realised that all that was beside the point right now. It was early in the morning and her nerves were jangled already from the prospect of starting her new job today. She needed to get her priorities sorted, and in the meantime she was still struggling with her bag.

Pulling in a deep breath, she said, 'I need your help to get him down from here. Between us we should be able to manage it. Just follow my instructions to the letter and we'll be fine.'

'No,' he said. 'Let me look at him. You did well to get to him, and be by his side, but I think it's probably best if I take over now and see what needs to be done. I'm a doctor. I saw what was happening and I came to do what I could for the child. I'll handle things from here.'

So he wasn't responsible for the site. That was something, anyway. She wondered briefly how they had both happened to arrive here at the same time. What were the chances of that? Still, it was unimportant right now. There were more pressing matters to deal with.

'We'll work together,' Sasha said. 'I'm a doctor, too, and I'll be glad of your help. If you reach behind me and open my medical bag you'll find a syringe and some gauze in there. I'll give him a painkilling injection, and then we'll sort out the best way to move him and stem the bleeding.' Ever since she had completed her training she had carried around the basic essentials she might need in an emergency, and she was thankful that she had taken that precaution now.

The man's grey eyes flickered momentarily in surprise as her words registered, but he made no comment except to nod briefly. He unclipped her bag and inspected the contents.

'Syringe,' he said, handing it to her after he had taken out a vial and drawn off the contents. 'As soon as that takes effect, we'll get him down from there.'

He glanced down at the boy and stroked his hair. 'We'll soon have you sorted, son. Just stay calm and let us do everything, OK?'

The boy nodded imperceptibly. 'I want my mum,' he whispered brokenly, and Sasha felt as though her heart was being wrenched in two. 'Will you get my mum?'

'We will,' the man said. 'Don't worry about that. Your sister has already called her and I'm sure she's on her way here right now.' He glanced at Sasha. 'I called the site manager, too. He should arrive at around the same time as the ambulance.'

He watched Casey's expression. 'Is the injection beginning to work? How do you feel?'

'It's not so bad now.' The child looked into his eyes and tried to swallow, and then said huskily, with the bluntness of youth, 'Am I going to die?'

'No, you're not going to die,' the man said seriously. He gave a faint smile. 'It's Monday, today. I never let my patients die on a Monday, especially when the sun's shining. We're going to take care of you. You're going to be just fine.'

Casey closed his eyes, as though the man's word was enough to reassure him. It must be wonderful to be able to inspire such confidence, Sasha thought. She gave him a second glance. Perhaps there was more to this man than she had at first acknowledged.

The boy's body went limp and Sasha quickly secured his airway and gave him oxygen via a ventilation bag. In the distance, she heard the sound of an ambulance siren. 'We should move him now,' she said. 'Are you ready?' She braced herself.

The man nodded, and they carefully eased the child off the metal strut. As soon as he was free, Sasha covered the wound with sterile gauze to stem the worst of the bleeding and strapped the dressing in place, while her helper supported the child.

By the time the ambulance arrived, she had secured intravenous access, and was giving Casey fluids to replace those he had lost and to lessen the shock to his system.

The man in charge of the building site came and opened up the gate so that the paramedics could stretcher the child out. Sasha and the man who had helped her went with them and watched as Casey was transferred to the ambulance.

The site manager looked worried. Sasha turned to him, and said, 'This should never have happened. The fencing needs to be replaced with something totally different. It isn't good enough to keep children out.'

'Yes, I see that. It's terrible what's gone on here,' he answered carefully, 'but, you know, the fencing was in perfectly good order. We're not responsible for any of this. We haven't broken any regulations.'

JOANNA NEIL 13

'That may be so, but what you're doing is obviously insufficient.'

'We have warning notices in place.'

'Yes, you do, but they weren't enough to stop curious children, were they?' Sasha pressed her point home. 'You have to do something more to keep them away.'

He gazed around him, at a loss. 'I'm not sure how much more I can do. Anyway, what was the boy doing here? I thought the Easter holidays were over now.'

'I expect the children are off school because there's a teachers' planning day today. But that isn't important, is it? The fence was never adequate, and really all this should be shielded off from children so that they're not tempted to come in here and explore.'

He shook his head in a doubtful gesture. 'I'll have to talk to the company bosses about that,' he said.

Sasha sent him a glittering blue glance. 'I hope you will,' she said, 'and I shall put in my own complaint. Something has to be done to stop this happening again... I'll do whatever I can to make sure that your bosses listen.'

By this time, the boy's mother had come hurrying to be with her child, and Sasha's attention was distracted for the moment. The doctor who had been helping her took the site manager to one side and she saw that he was having a quiet word with him. She couldn't make out what was being said, but the manager appeared to be in a subdued frame of mind.

'What happened?' the woman asked, her face pale with anxiety. 'Is Casey going to be all right?'

'He'll need surgery,' Sasha told her. 'There's a possibility that his spleen is ruptured, and the surgeon will need to check for internal injuries and repair the damage. We've done what we can to stabilise his condition and I hope that we've lessened the chances of any more problems occurring. You can be assured that he's going to be in good hands from now on.'

'Thank you for what you've done. You and your friend have been so good.' The woman looked distraught. She glanced around to where the paramedics were making final preparations. 'I have to go. I need to be with my son, but I just wanted to tell you how much I appreciate what you did. They've said my daughter and I can ride in the ambulance with him. Thank you so much.'

'You're welcome.'

Sasha watched the ambulance move away, and trusted that things would go well for them. She felt empty inside, deflated somehow. It had been a bad start to the day, and she was feeling shaken up and out of sorts. On her way to her first day in a new job she could have wished that things had gone better.

'Are you all right?'

She glanced up and realised with a start that the doctor was studying her, his grey eyes travelling over her features as though he would seek out her innermost thoughts.

'I'm fine,' she said, getting a grip on herself. She grimaced. 'My hair feels as though it's full of brick dust and my clothes are grimy, but other than that I'm just fine.'

He gave her a wry smile, his glance moving over the mass of chestnut curls that spilled down to her shoulders and then trailing over her slender frame. She was wearing a cotton top that fitted snugly and a suede skirt that gently skimmed her hips. 'I expect the dust will brush off eventually.'

His expression sobered. 'You know, you really should have waited for the emergency services to arrive. For one thing, it was foolhardy to try to help him on your own. Besides that, you put yourself in danger, and if something had gone wrong, there would have been two casualties for the paramedics to deal with. It was reckless of you to rush into action.' He looked her over once more. 'As it is, you didn't escape entirely, did you? You've a nasty cut. You had better let me take a look at that.'

He was staring at her leg, and she glanced down and saw that blood had congealed on her ankle.

'It's nothing,' she muttered. His comments stung her a little. What right did he have to tell her how to go on? 'I'll deal with it myself in a little while. I'm sure you must have other things that you need to be doing.' She added stiffly, 'I don't think it would have been a good idea to wait for the ambulance. The boy could have died without immediate treatment. Besides, I don't recall seeing you hanging around, twiddling your thumbs.'

He gave a half-smile. 'But I'm a man, and I'm used to working under difficult conditions. I trained with the air-sea rescue teams, and I've had a lot of years of experience. You're just a slip of a girl and you look as though a puff of wind would blow you over…' His glance flicked downwards. 'Besides that, your footwear is hardly suitable for exercises like the one you just took on. With heels like that, you were almost bound to rick your ankle.'

She sent him a withering stare. 'But I didn't. It's just a gash, that's all. I'm a lot stronger than I look, and I'm perfectly capable of coping with difficult situations.'

'If you say so.' He didn't look too sure of that and he glanced once again at her ankle, before shrugging his shoulders and adding, 'You're an independent soul, aren't you? Not afraid to speak your mind. Perhaps too much so. The site manager is feeling quite anxious after what you said to him.'

'Good. Perhaps something will be done about securing the site properly.'

'Oh, I'm sure it will…though, to be absolutely fair, he was right when he said they had done nothing wrong.' His mouth made a crooked slant. 'I added my two-pennyworth, and told him it wouldn't look good for the company if news of what happened here was to leak out to the local press. I think he got the message, and he's promised to sort things out.'

. 'Well, that's good news.' She gave him a brief smile. At least something was going right.

His gaze narrowed on her. 'You know, you did a tremendous job today, but I'm not sure that you'll always get what you want by going at it like a bull at a gate. Do you always insist on taking charge or going it alone?'

'Mostly,' she admitted, giving him a sideways glance. Who was he to criticise her way of doing things? 'I've usually found that I get on better that way.'

It was more a question of having little choice in the matter, she thought ruefully. Her life had always been a balance between looking out for herself and her younger brother, and making sure that her mother was all right. No one had been there to take up the burden for her, and now she shouldered the responsibility automatically. It had become a way of life.

Even though her brother had turned twenty now and was in his first year at university, he was still struggling and often came to her for help. Just now, he was worrying about his exams, afraid that he wasn't going to do very well, and she couldn't help thinking that there was more he was keeping from her. As to her mother, she had never been strong, and now that she was ill again, Sasha had more to lose sleep over. Sometimes she wished things could be different, that she didn't have to bear her worries on her own, but it wasn't to be, and she simply managed the best way she could.

She didn't say any of that to this stranger, though. 'Thank you for helping me,' she said with a smile. 'I'm glad you came along when you did, or it could have been really awkward.' She paused. 'I don't know your name. I feel that I should, given what we've just been through.'

'Matt,' he said. 'It's Matthew, but everyone calls me Matt.'

'I'm Sasha,' she told him. 'Thanks again for stopping to help.' She hesitated. 'I'll let you get on your way. I'm sure I must be keeping you from something.'

He glanced at the watch on his wrist. 'If you're certain that you're all right… I do have somewhere I should be right now—an important meeting—and I'm going to be late as it is. But make sure you clean up that ankle. It looks like a nasty gash, and it could become infected.'

'I'll deal with it,' she said, and he nodded and walked away from her, going over to the side of the road to unlock a sleek, midnight-blue saloon. She waited as he drove off, and wondered why it was that their paths had crossed at all. It was lucky for Casey that they had, but she guessed that would be the last she would see of the good-looking doctor.

It was probably just as well. He had a way of taking the wind out of her sails, and she wasn't one to enjoy being stopped in her tracks.

She went back to her car and set off for the hospital. She was already late, and she needed time to clean up. It wasn't a good start for her new post in A and E.

'So you're the new doctor. Dr Rushford, is it? We wondered what had happened to you,' a fair-haired nurse said when Sasha finally made an appearance in the emergency room. 'We thought perhaps you had changed your mind about the job.' She laughed. 'To be honest, I wouldn't have blamed you—we get rushed off our feet sometimes, and we don't know whether we're coming or going. I'm Amanda, by the way.'

'Hello, Amanda.' Sasha smiled at her. 'You can call me Sasha. I'm sorry I'm late. I did phone to say that I'd been delayed. I had to stop and help a little boy who was injured on a building site. It was unavoidable, I'm afraid.'

'Oh, you must mean Casey. He was admitted a while ago. He's in surgery right this minute. I think he's going to be all right, from all accounts. Mr Danby, our surgeon, reckons he can patch him up. You did a good job.'

'I'm glad things are turning out better for the boy.' Sasha glanced around. 'I should get started and make up for lost time. Where am I needed?'

'Over in treatment bay number two. It's our paediatric bay. Nathan will show you the ropes. He's our senior house officer, and he's looking after the children who are admitted today. We're really glad to have you with us. It's been hard to find permanent grade staff to fill the posts. We're snowed under with work.'

'Thanks, Amanda. I'll do my best to help out.'

Sasha worked with Nathan for the rest of the morning. He was a cheerful soul, who made the children smile even when they were feeling poorly or hurt, and she guessed she was going to enjoy working here. She just hoped her boss was going to be as amenable as everyone else, but so far she hadn't met him.

'Where's the consultant in charge?' she asked Nathan. 'I haven't seen him yet.'

'Dr Benton? He's treating a couple of road accident victims,' Nathan told her. 'I expect he'll catch up with you a bit later on.'

It was easy to get along with Nathan, Sasha discovered. In between dealing with patients, he showed her where all the equipment was kept and took her on a whistle-stop tour of the department.

'What do you think?' he asked. 'Are you happy with everything?'

'I've seen a lot of really good things this morning,' she said, 'especially the way the staff interact, and the way they deal with patients.'

'I sense a *but* in there,' Nathan said. 'Was there something you didn't like?'

'Well…' She hesitated for a moment, and then went on, 'To be honest, I was surprised to see that children are treated alongside adults. It's really unsettling for some of them. The boy with the fractured arm was very unhappy. Disregarding the fact that he was shocked and in pain, he was frightened by everything that was going on around him…all the equipment, the noise, the whole atmosphere seemed to faze him, even though the staff did their best to put him at ease.'

'It's always been like that here…as long as I've worked here, anyway. I don't think there's the money available for changing things.'

'There's always something that can be done, surely?' Sasha said firmly. 'I don't believe that things can't be changed. Nothing has to be set in stone. And as to the way parents are excluded from the treatment bay—I don't think that's a good idea.' She wondered belatedly if she was saying too much, too soon. She was a newcomer here after all.

Nathan grimaced. 'You're a paediatrician... I expect you've had more experience of how these things work best. I'm not sure how much change we can put into place, though.'

'Because of your consultant? Would he object?'

Nathan opened his mouth to answer, but stopped himself. They were standing in the arched recess of the treatment bay, and the noise of a curtain being briskly swished aside caught Sasha's attention and caused her to swing around.

'Are you having a go at the system here now, Sasha?' a familiar voice said. 'Haven't you tried to put the world to rights enough for one day? You've only been here five minutes and already you're wanting to reorganise the department.'

Sasha stared as a grey-suited man emerged from the cubicle. It was the doctor who had helped her out with Casey earlier that day. Her mouth went dry and she felt oddly out of synch all at once, as though she had been suddenly knocked for six.

'What are you doing here?' she asked, when she had herself together once more. 'I thought you worked for air-sea rescue.'

'That was some time ago.' Matt gave a humourless smile, a faint twisting of his mouth. 'I'm the consultant in charge here, and I wasn't expecting to see you turn up in my department. Heaven forbid I should be landed with a revolutionary activist on my team. What did I do to deserve that?'

'Do you two know each other?' Nathan looked from one to the other with a bemused air.

'We met this morning, when I was on my way to the management meeting,' Matt said.

'Ah, that explains it.' Nathan smiled. He started to walk away. 'I'll leave you to get reacquainted while I go and check on the results of some blood tests.'

Matt cast a glance over Sasha, his grey gaze flicking over her burnished hair. 'I must say you clean up pretty well. The way things were earlier, I might have been confronted with a dust bomb.'

She sent him a disdainful look. 'I took advantage of the shower room here. I was late already, but I figured it would be best all round if I started off feeling better about myself.' Her gaze dared him to object, but he didn't comment on what she had said. He simply looked at her as though she was a fairly odd species, someone alien to his world.

He said shortly, 'So, you have a problem with the way the department operates? Is there anything else you find disagreeable? We might as well clear the air while you're in full critical mode.'

'I didn't mean to be critical,' she said, backtracking. 'I was just expressing an opinion. I didn't realise that I was treading on any toes.'

'You aren't. I'm interested in hearing people's views.'

'Really?' She was sceptical. He didn't look as

though he was going to listen favourably to what she had to say. 'Some other time, perhaps.'

'As you please.' His grey eyes narrowed. 'It's probably a wise decision. There are patients desperately in need of attention. No doubt they'll value your assistance.'

He walked away from her, and Sasha was left to gaze after him, wondering how she could have managed to make such a mess of things so early on.

'Are you OK?' Nathan returned to her side and gave her a searching look. 'Did you have a run-in with Matt? I couldn't help hearing some of what he said. He can be a bit challenging sometimes.'

'No…everything's fine.' She was hesitant about saying anything more. She was new here, and she'd already said too much and burned her boats. In fact, sometimes she wished she could bite off her tongue before it ran away with her.

'He was hard on you, considering this is your first day. He hasn't been here all that long himself, and we're all still getting used to him.'

'He was OK. I should learn to think before I speak. I'm always putting my foot in it… I tend to say what's on my mind before I've operated my brain. Besides, I didn't get off to a very good beginning today, with coming in late.'

'Matt's been a bit short with everyone lately. I imagine something's on his mind—trouble at home, perhaps.'

'He was fine, no problem.' Sasha gave Nathan a brief smile and went to find her next patient. So Matt

Benton had things on his mind, did he? Didn't everyone?

Her own problems crowded in on her. Her mother was ill, and her brother was going through some sort of crisis, and now she had landed herself in trouble on her first day at work. How was she going to put that situation right?

Matt Benton was her boss, and she had crossed swords with him before she had even got to know him. She made a wry face. There was no way out. She was doomed.

CHAPTER TWO

'HI, SASHA. I'm sorry to ring so early in the morning, but I wanted to catch you before you left for work.'

'That's all right, Sam. Is there a problem?' Her brother sounded low, and Sasha was immediately on the alert.

'Nothing to worry about. It's just that I left a textbook behind when I came home for the Easter holidays. I wondered if you could get it to me somehow? Perhaps give it to my friend, Tom? He said he was coming over here to pick up some of his things today, and he could bring it to me. I need it so that I can study for the exams.' He paused. 'I hope I'm not putting you to too much trouble. I know how busy you are with the new job and everything.'

'That's all right. I'll see if I can drop it at his house on my way to work. Is everything all right with you?' She knew her brother well enough, and something in his voice bothered her.

'I'm OK. I'm a bit worried about the exams—there's a lot of work, and I don't seem to be getting on very well. The book might help.'

Sasha frowned. That wasn't like Sam. He was a good student, quick and clever, and he had always been keen to study pharmacy. There was probably more to it than he was saying. 'Are you getting enough rest? You need a fresh mind if you're trying to learn stuff. I know you're doing a part-time job in the union bar as well. Perhaps you need to cut down on your hours.'

'Can't do that. I need the money. Anyway, I'll be fine. Don't worry.' He hesitated again, then asked, 'How's Mum? She didn't look too well when I was home. Is it a virus, do you think, or a problem with her medication?'

'I'm not sure. It may be a virus. She's still not feeling too good, but there's nothing specific to say it's this or that, and her doctor can't pin it down to anything just yet. She says there shouldn't be any problem with the medication because her response to it is constantly monitored, so for the time being she's advised her to rest. I've arranged for a neighbour— Theresa—to look in on her and let me know if there's a problem. You know her, don't you? She's still home from university just now, and she said it was no trouble.'

'Theresa's OK. She's young, but she's reliable, isn't she?' Sam was thoughtful for a moment or two. 'I hoped that moving to be nearer the coast would be good for Mum, but it hasn't worked out that way, has it?'

'Give it time. We've only been here for a couple of months. Let's see how things go.'

He rang off a short time later, and Sasha went to look in on her mother. She was in bed, resting, and Sasha could see from the tray on her bedside table that her breakfast was only partly touched.

'Didn't you like the egg?' Sasha asked, looking at the breakfast tray doubtfully. 'Is there something different you'd like me to get for you?'

'Nothing, Sasha, thanks.' Her mother smiled, and leaned back against her pillows. Her face was pale, a stark contrast to the dark brown of her hair. 'The breakfast was lovely, but I'm not very hungry today. I think I'll just close my eyes for a while. I'm very tired. I'm sorry to be such a nuisance.'

'You mustn't talk like that.' Sasha clasped her mother's hand in hers. 'You're not a nuisance, and you just have to rest and get better.' She grimaced. 'I wish I could stay with you, but I have to go in to work. I've asked Theresa to come and be with you. You get on well with her, don't you? She's writing up her notes for university, so she'll be downstairs if you need her, and you know my phone number at the hospital. If you feel worse or you need me, give me a ring.'

'Bless you, I'll be fine.' Her mother patted her hand. 'You just concentrate on your job. You need to find a way to get on with that new boss of yours.'

'Now, that's a tall order.' Sasha gave her mother an answering smile. She had been working with Matt for a couple of weeks now, and she was no nearer to finding out what made him tick. He ran the department with a determined hand. Things were done the way he wanted, and he was single-minded, focused on achieving each target he set. 'I mean it—ring me if you need me. I'll be in a meeting this afternoon for a while, but you can still call me. They'll find me easily enough.'

Just a short time later, Sasha arrived at the hospital. It was all go, right from the start, and for the most part she was kept busy dealing with small children who had been injured at home, in the house or playing in the garden. Later that morning, though, a boy was brought in by ambulance, accompanied by a teacher from his school.

Sasha went to examine him. The paramedics were bringing him in on a trolley, and she listened to their report as they wheeled him to the treatment bay. He was about nine years old, and he was suffering from chest pain and breathlessness.

'He was concussed,' the paramedic said. 'He's been vomiting, and he was very dizzy to begin with.'

'OK. Thank you,' Sasha murmured, and the paramedic left.

Sasha turned to the woman teacher, who was looking concerned. 'Can you tell me what happened to the boy?'

'We were on a school trip…at a farm, with a riding stable.' She winced. 'It was all going really well to begin with. The children were able to ride on the horses, but then Ryan slipped away from his teacher and went inside the stables to see the animals being groomed. One of the horses must have been frightened by something and he kicked out. From what I heard, Ryan was too close, and he was kicked in the chest. I think he must have banged his head as he fell.'

'Have his parents been contacted?'

'Yes. They were coming straight here. They should have arrived by now.'

'Good. I'll go and examine him more thoroughly.' She glanced at the teacher. 'Are you going back to the school now?'

'I thought I'd wait for a while, to make sure that he's all right.' She gave Sasha a worried look.

'That's all right. I'll be able to let you know more later,' Sasha said. 'If you go with the nurse, she'll show you where you can wait.' She glanced at Amanda for confirmation, and the nurse nodded and led the woman away, talking to her quietly as they went towards the visitors' room.

In the treatment bay, Sasha drew the curtain around the cubicle and spoke quietly to the boy. 'I'm going to have a quick look at your injuries,' she told him. 'I'll be as careful as I can so as not to hurt you any more. That must have been a nasty kick the horse gave you. I think you've probably broken a rib or two, but I just need to be sure there is no other damage.'

Ryan was upset, crying quietly, but he nodded as though he understood. 'I want my mum and dad,' he said.

'I know. I'll see if I can find them for you in a minute. I just want to make sure that you're going to be all right first.'

Suddenly, though, the boy's face paled, and he collapsed, slumping back against his pillows. Sasha moved fast, calling for assistance, getting ready to intubate him. Matt came into the cubicle along with a nurse, and Sasha felt a qualm of uncertainty. She hadn't expected Matt to come and watch over her.

She carefully passed an endotracheal tube into the boy's windpipe and set up the ventilation equipment.

'I think there must be blood in the pleural cavity,' she said to Matt. Turning to the nurse, she added, 'Now that he's on oxygen, let's get a chest X-ray so that we can see what's happened. We'll do a CT scan of his head as well, just to make sure that he's not fractured anything.'

The X-ray was done in double-quick time and showed a shadowing. Matt frowned. 'You were right,' he said, inspecting the film with Sasha. 'That's a haemothorax.'

'It certainly looks like it,' Sasha acknowledged. 'I'm going to insert two cannulae and send blood for cross-matching. We'll give him intravenous fluids and then I'll put in a chest drain to reduce the pressure on his lung.'

'You'll need an analgesic, then,' the nurse said.

Sasha nodded, and the nurse hurried to get what was needed. Sasha was already cleaning the skin of the boy's chest and identifying the intercostal space. When the nurse came back, Sasha quickly inserted a chest drain and connected it to an underwater seal.

'That looks good,' Matt said after a minute or two.

Sasha nodded and said to the nurse, 'I'll suture the drain in place and then perhaps you could cover it with a dressing and tape.'

'I will. Are you going to X-ray the chest again afterwards?' the nurse asked.

'Yes, as soon as we've finished, we'll X-ray to confirm that the drain is in place properly.'

When the boy came round just a little while later, he looked confused and frightened. He looked at the equipment and the monitors that flashed and blinked, and his eyes widened. Sasha could see that he was upset.

'Don't worry about any of those things,' she said gently. 'They're just there so that we can make sure that everything's all right.'

'Where is my mum?'

'I think she's in the waiting room,' Sasha said. 'I'll find out for you.'

'But I want to see her now.' His chest started to heave and his face crumpled with the pain of exertion.

'Just you sit back and try to relax,' Sasha said soothingly. 'I'll go and find your mother, I promise. You're doing very well. You've been very brave.'

He relaxed a little, and when she was sure that he was in no danger, Sasha left him in the care of the nurse while she went to find Amanda. Matt stayed with the boy, and she saw that he was talking quietly to him.

Amanda was by the desk. 'Do you know where Ryan's parents are?' Sasha asked. 'I heard that they had arrived, but they didn't come into the treatment room. The child is making himself ill by being upset.'

'They're in the waiting room,' Amanda said. 'We're not allowed to bring them into the treatment room. They wanted to come in, but it's policy. It's something we've always done here, even before Matt came to take charge.' Her glance slanted sideways and Sasha saw that Matt had come to join them.

Sasha frowned. 'I'd prefer it if they were allowed in,' she said. 'I think it's better for the children, and it makes them feel more secure.'

Matt met her glance steadily. 'We believe that they can make matters worse, and sometimes they get in the way.'

'I don't think that's a valid argument,' she told him, her tone stiffening.

'Really? We've had some experience of this, you know. All sorts of problems can crop up when the parents are involved.'

'Don't you think that's a very negative attitude to take? If they caused a problem of any kind, they could be asked to leave.' Her blue eyes flashed. 'While I'm treating children, I'd prefer it if the parents were with them. I'm sorry if that doesn't fit in with your rules, but it's the way I like to work.'

He said calmly, 'Yes, I see that. I also see that you're very young, and full of ideas, and I understand that you're fired up with the need to change everything. You've only been here a short time, though, and at the moment the system doesn't work that way. I hardly think this is the time or place to change management decisions. Perhaps we should discuss this later?'

He glanced obliquely at Amanda, and Sasha immediately felt chastened. He was right. She was quarrelling with him in front of a colleague, and it simply wouldn't do.'

'Of course,' she said flatly. 'Perhaps we can arrange a time that would suit.'

He nodded. 'We have a meeting scheduled for permanent grade staff this afternoon. I imagine we can talk then.'

Her chin lifted. 'That's fine by me. If you'll excuse me, I need to go and talk to Ryan's parents and arrange for them to see him.' At the same time, she would update the teacher on his condition so that she could report back to the school.

When the time came for the meeting that afternoon, Matt was called away to take a phone call at the reception desk. Sasha was already there, writing up her case notes in preparation for the handover to her replacement.

'I'll be along to take the meeting in a few minutes,' Matt told her. 'When you go to the conference room, if I'm not through in time, ask everyone to get a coffee and chat among themselves for a while, would you?'

'I will. I'll just finish these notes first.'

The notes didn't take long, but she couldn't help overhear snatches of his conversation with whoever was on the other end of the line. If it had bothered him that she might hear, surely he could have taken the call on a different phone? As it was, Sasha gathered that someone had been taken ill, and that he had to make arrangements for a little boy to be picked up from nursery school.

She stopped what she was doing for a moment. Was he married? It hadn't occurred to her that he might have a wife and child at home, and for some reason the idea troubled her.

It was none of her business of course, but when he put the phone down and dialled another number, she was curious.

'Hello, Dad,' he said. 'Have I called you at a bad time?' There was a pause and then he went on, 'I wondered if you could pick Josh up from nursery school for me? I'm still on duty and it's going to be awkward for me to get there in time.' He paused. 'Yes, that's right. I'll do my best to get to you as soon as I can. I know you have appointments to keep. No, I haven't had any word from Helen yet. It's worrying.' He pulled a face. 'I've no idea where she is.'

Sasha filled in the last section of her notes and filed the charts away. It felt wrong to be listening in to his conversation and she tried to blank it out.

Matt was still on the phone when she went to the conference room, and she set about organising coffee for everyone as he had asked, and then she went and talked to Nathan and Amanda for a while.

Amanda said quietly, 'I'm sorry you had a run-in with Matt earlier. I imagine he'll take on board what you're saying, if you give him time. You perhaps caught him at a bad moment. From what I hear, he's very keen to see that things run smoothly. He's worked in a number of hospitals before this one, and each one has been a step on the way to making him a consultant. I don't think he's come to where he is now without listening to people and making changes.'

'I expect you're right. I should have tackled things differently.'

'He's good at his job,' Nathan put in. 'I just wonder what his next goal will be…a hospital where the emergency department is bigger, I imagine, and where the responsibility increases proportionally.'

When Matt finally came into the room, Sasha thought he seemed preoccupied. Even so, he opened the meeting briskly and went through the business in hand in a smoothly efficient manner. He was so focused now that she doubted anyone else would have guessed that he had things on his mind.

At the end, he asked if there were any matters to be raised, and one or two people had something to say. Even though he was under pressure, Matt dealt carefully with each point until people were satisfied with the conclusion. Sasha wondered whether she should add her bit. She was a newcomer, though, and maybe she ought not to rock the boat. And anyway, it might be the wrong time to say anything if Matt was having problems at home. Was Helen his wife? Had she left him? She still wasn't sure why that bothered her.

'Dr Rushford? Sasha?' Matt's voice cut in on her thoughts. 'Wasn't there something you wanted to say?'

She looked up at him in consternation. 'Oh…' Her attention had been wandering, and now his direct approach took her by surprise. 'I'm not sure…perhaps some other time would be better?'

He shook his head. 'I understood that you had one

or two concerns. It's probably best if we get them out into the open. Let's deal with any worries you have right now.'

He wasn't leaving her any choice, was he? His grey eyes watched her steadily and she straightened in her seat. He must have known she hadn't been listening to what was going on.

She said hesitantly, 'Well, if you insist, there is something I'd like to query.' She lifted her chin a fraction. 'It's the question of the way our paediatric care is organised. I'm not sure that it's the best we can do for the children we treat.'

Matt's dark brows rose expressively. 'You think we're going about everything the wrong way?'

She grimaced. Was he trying to put her down in front of all these people? Uncomfortable now, she shifted in her chair, smoothing down her narrow-fitting skirt in a faintly nervous gesture. His eyes followed the movement, his gaze lingering on the shapeliness of her long legs.

She stilled her hands. 'I didn't say that.' She straightened her shoulders. 'A lot of what we're doing is very good, but I think there are some elements that could be improved.'

His grey eyes glittered, piercing her like a lance. 'What did you have in mind, exactly?'

'Well, for instance, I think we should have a completely separate wing for children's emergency care, and the staff who work there ought to be specialised in treating children. At the moment they are looked after in the same area as adults, and it's scary for them. The equipment all around is frightening, and the fact that adults are treated close by is upsetting.'

'I think you've mentioned this before,' Matt said. 'We do have them in a bay that is set apart from the adult treatment bay.'

'I appreciate that, but it isn't far enough away for them to be unaware of what's going on.'

'We're a busy hospital, with many departments. Perhaps you don't realise that we have problems with space here.'

'I know space is limited,' she said in a curt tone, 'but I'm sure somewhere suitable could be found in a hospital this size. I'm not asking for a new building, just better use of resources.'

'Those resources also include staff, and we already have a problem with recruitment. There have been occasions, before my time as consultant here but still fairly recently, when the A and E department has been threatened with closure at certain times at night because we haven't been able to cope with demand.' He threw her a challenging look. 'How do you propose we deal with that?'

'There must be solutions,' she countered, 'alternatives that haven't been explored.'

'Do you think so?' Matt was sceptical. 'Believe me, we've had endless meetings on the subject. I've only been here for a few months, but I've discussed this with the hospital management and they assure me everything that can be done has been done.'

'I'm sure I can think up a few options that haven't been tried.'

His expression was something to see. 'Is that so?' His mouth made an odd shape, hovering somewhere between amusement and exasperation.

She grimaced. He thought she was simply young and inexperienced, and that her views could be discounted. He would have to learn that there was more to her than that. She said tightly, 'For instance, we could instigate a positive recruitment drive with incentives for potential new staff members. I've looked into some of the measures that have been taken, and I think we could make some improvements.'

'Is that so? You seem very sure of yourself.'

She grimaced. 'I'm simply trying to be constructive. Would you like me to go through some of my suggestions now?'

He glanced at his watch. 'I don't think we have the time at the moment. Some of us have to be back on duty.' He gave her a brief, taut smile. 'Perhaps you could put your ideas down on paper and let me have them on my desk. I'll go through them with you at the first opportunity.'

She nodded, unsure what to make of him. 'I'll do that.'

'Good.' He glanced around the room. 'That's it for now, everyone. If you'll excuse me, I have to leave right away. I have a pressing appointment. I'll see you all tomorrow.'

People began to push back chairs, shuffle papers and gradually make their way out of the room. Sasha sat for a moment, a little shaken by her set-to with Matt. Had she actually taken on a consultant, espe-

cially one who was so highly thought of by all the
hospital chiefs? He was energetic and gifted with a
quick mind, and everyone respected the drive and am-
bition that had brought him to this position at such a
young age. What had she been thinking of, taking him
on? To be fair, he had provoked her, otherwise she
would never have stood up to him in a room full of
people.

'Are you all right?' Nathan came and stood beside
her as she gathered up her bag and started towards
the door. 'You look a bit subdued.'

She sent him a fleeting smile. 'I'm fine. I think
perhaps I should have kept quiet. I probably made a
fool of myself. I'm so used to saying what I think
and trying to sort things out. I've always done it, all
my life.' She'd had to. At first it had been a way of
compensating for the insecurities of her youth…she'd
learned to stand on her own two feet, to take care of
her younger brother and fight his corner…and now
she didn't know any other way.

'He was a bit tough on you, I thought. He's so used
to doing things his way, and that's probably why he's
made his way up the career ladder so fast, I reckon.
Amanda had a point in what she said earlier… I heard
he'd blitzed his way through his last few hospital appointments to become consultant. There's no stopping
him. He goes after what he wants and then he moves
on.'

He made a wry face. 'Even so, he doesn't usually
go head to head with new people like that. He's been
a bit tense lately—something must be happening at

home, I reckon.' Nathan's mouth made an odd shape. 'I heard that he's having to look after a four-year-old. The child's mother walked out on him.'

Sasha stared at him in horror. 'That's awful. How on earth can he be managing? Does he have any help? What about his family? Can they do anything?'

Nathan shrugged. 'I don't know all the details. I think his mother died many years ago, but his father's still around. He's semi-retired now, but he still works part time as a GP. I don't know about any other family.'

Sasha frowned. 'I can't think of anything worse. How can this have come about? Matt must be beside himself with worry. What kind of mother abandons her child?'

Nathan didn't answer. Sasha glanced at him, and his expression was odd, guilty, like a dog caught tearing at the family rug. She turned and saw the object of his dismay.

Matt had come back into the room and was retrieving some papers for his briefcase. He directed a furious stare her way.

'Don't you have anything better to do than gossip about my private life?'

She opened her mouth to say something, but nothing came out. Nathan said quickly, 'I'm sorry. We didn't mean anything by it. We were just saying that sometimes it can be difficult to balance work and home. I'm lucky. I just share a flat with friends, and I don't have any particular stresses to get in the way.

I think Sasha has a difficult home life, too, one way and another.'

'I'm sure she doesn't need you to defend her.' Matt glared at him. 'Shouldn't you be back on duty?'

Nathan nodded, looking abashed. 'I'm just on my way now.' He sent Sasha a worried glance, and she tried to give him a reassuring smile. It came out all wrong, like a pale imitation, but he nodded and hurried away towards A and E.

Matt slid the papers into his briefcase and snapped the clasp shut. He made to stride away, but Sasha suddenly came to her senses and dashed after him.

'I'm sorry,' she said, touching his arm to get his attention. His head turned and he looked down to where her hand rested on his jacket sleeve and he frowned.

She went on quickly, 'I really didn't mean to talk about you behind your back. I couldn't help hearing something of what you said on the telephone, and I thought perhaps you must have a lot on your mind. It must be difficult, having to take care of a small child on your own. If I can help in any way, I will...you only have to ask.'

'Why on earth would I need your help?' His grey eyes were dark and impenetrable, and she felt utterly foolish and out of her depth.

She said faintly, 'I just think it does no good to bottle things up. If you have a problem, it can be helpful to share it with someone. I don't know how I would cope if I was suddenly landed with a child to care for, and the circumstances must be dreadful. I can't understand how any mother could simply leave her child behind.'

His eyes narrowed. 'You don't know when to stop, do you? You glide out onto thin ice, without any regard for how dangerous it might be. Are you mad?'

'I'm sorry.' She backed away, looking desolate. He had a point, didn't he? What was wrong with her? Why did she have to wade in and offer help where it wasn't wanted? 'You're right, it's nothing to do with me. I don't know what I was thinking. I won't say another word on the subject.'

He glowered at her. 'I wouldn't make promises you can't possibly keep, if I were you,' he said with dry sarcasm. 'I doubt you have any idea how to restrain yourself.'

His mouth made a hard line. 'Just so you don't go giving anyone the wrong idea, perhaps I should put you right on a few things.'

He moved closer and she took a step backwards, worried by his grim expression. 'You don't have to,' she said.

'I think I do. This could get out of hand.' He grimaced. 'Just to get things clear, the child is my sister's boy, and unfortunately my sister is ill.'

'I'm sorry.'

'So am I. She's having a mental breakdown because things have gone wrong in her life. Unfortunately she's taken it into her head that she's no good for her child, and that he'll be better off without her. That is why she's gone off and left him.

She's a good woman and I don't want to hear a bad word about her.'

'You're right. I shouldn't have made judgements.'

'No, you shouldn't.' His expression was like a thundercloud. 'You do not repeat any of this, to anyone. Have I made myself perfectly clear?'

She nodded, not daring to speak.

'Good,' he said, his tone brisk. 'I'm glad we've settled that.' He sent her a fulminating glance. 'I don't want to hear even a hint that you've been talking to anyone else about this. This is my business and no one else's. Are we quite definite about that?'

She nodded again. 'Yes, I understand. I'm sorry.'

He walked away without saying another word, and Sasha stared after him. His anger was a potent thing, and frightening to see. Why did she get herself into these scrapes? All she wanted to do was to help—and the thought of that poor child having to come to terms with his mother's disappearance was almost unbearable to contemplate. He must be desperately unhappy. How could a child that young even begin to understand what was going on?

She knew only too well what it was like to be abandoned by a parent, and for her brother it must have been even worse. Sam had been very young when their mother had succumbed to illness and their father had left them to fend for themselves. She knew just how devastating an effect that could have on a young child.

If only she could do something to help Matt and his small nephew… It was an impossible situation to be in, though, wasn't it? Matt was angry with her, and would reject any move she made. He didn't want her help. He had made that very clear.

She had messed things up all over again. Would she never learn?

CHAPTER THREE

'THANKS for coming in again, Theresa. I don't know how I would have managed without your help this last couple of days.' Sasha gave the girl a quick smile. 'Are you sure that I'm not putting too much on you?'

Theresa shook her head. Beams of light shone through the kitchen window, dancing over her fair hair, so that the soft waves shimmered. 'I have some time off university for my study days, and it makes no difference to me whether I study at home or here. Your mother's a lovely lady—she's no trouble at all.' She frowned slightly, her grey eyes troubled. 'Is she still not feeling any better?'

Sasha shook her head. 'I thought perhaps she had a virus, and that she might start to recover if she had some rest in bed for a few days, but she seems to be getting worse. She has a temperature and now she's starting to cough. I've asked the doctor to call in and see her, so if you could ring me and let me know what she has to say, I'll be very grateful.' Sasha winced. 'I wanted to take time off work to stay with her myself, but Mum won't hear of it. She was threatening to get out of bed, so we decided on a compromise. She'll let the doctor take a look at her, as long as I go on as normal.'

Theresa smiled. 'That sounds like your mother.

She's very sweet, but she can be determined when she wants, can't she?'

'Too right.'

'What do you think is wrong with her? I know she was ill for a long time some years back. Is it something to do with that same illness?'

Sasha shook her head. 'I don't think so. I hope not. I think it's probably a chest infection of some kind. She's been overdoing things lately—she wanted to decorate the house soon after we moved in, to make it more our own—and I suspect her immune system is low as a result. I asked the doctor to give her antibiotics, but she thought it was a virus to begin with, and preferred to wait a while.'

Theresa grimaced. 'It's a worry for you, isn't it? I'll give you a call when the doctor's been to see her, and I'll let you know if there's any problem at all.'

'Thanks, Theresa. I'll go and say goodbye to her, and then I must rush off to work.' She was torn, wanting to stay with her mother and make sure that everything was all right, and at the same time she knew that if she was late, Matt would have something to say about it. She hadn't got off to the best of starts with him, and it was still early days yet. The job was important to her. At the very least, it kept a roof over their heads.

By the time she reached A and E, she was already feeling under pressure. Her mother's breathing had been laboured, and Sasha was convinced that antibiotics would help.

Despite her worries, though, she tried to put on a

cheerful face for her patients. Children picked up on every little signal, and she wanted to make sure that everything about their care went smoothly.

In her coffee-break, she started to put pictures up on the wall, happy scenes of colourful boats sailing on blue oceans, and birds hovering overhead, inspecting what was going on.

'You're quite set on changing things around here, aren't you?' Matt said, giving her a quizzical look as he walked by the paediatric bay. He stopped to see what she was doing.

She threw him a quick glance. He made an impressive figure, smartly dressed in an expensively tailored dark suit that emphasised his strong, lean frame. His jaw was clean-cut, and his grey eyes danced with curious lights as he checked her over.

He was far too good-looking for her peace of mind. Somehow he managed to make her heart thump whenever he was close by, and that was disconcerting in itself. It was probably simply down to worry that he was about to find something wrong in whatever she was planning to do. She tried to ignore those unsettling feelings and concentrate instead on arranging the pictures, but she was conscious all the time of his gaze on her.

He turned his attention to the display. 'Isn't that one a bit askew?'

'Is it? If you have time to stand there and find fault, you could lend a hand,' she answered shortly. 'Better still, you could arrange for someone to come in and paint a few murals for us. That would be a boost for the children.'

'I imagine it would make a big dent in the budget, too,' he said, his mouth making a crooked line. 'Last I heard, we were spending more money than we had available.'

'I expect there's a charitable institution that could organise something.' She sent him a direct glance. 'You could look into it.'

'I could,' he said. 'If I had any time to spare.' He grimaced. 'Right now I have a patient to attend to, and as soon as I've dealt with him I'm expected to attend a management meeting.'

'Life is so full, isn't it?' She shot him a look of sympathy that was patently insincere, and his eyes narrowed on her, threatening retribution.

He walked away, though, and she saw him disappear into one of the adult treatment cubicles. She made a face. Clearly he didn't rate spending time or money on anything that wasn't to do with immediate patient care, and she had her work cut out if she wanted to get him to change his mind.

She was still smarting over his lack of interest when a small child was brought in some time later. Nathan came to help her.

'I thought you might want some support,' he said. 'I saw you and Matt having another skirmish. You shouldn't let him bother you.'

'I won't.' She said it firmly enough, but in her mind she wasn't so sure.

She went over to the child. The boy was three or

four years old, and he was sobbing quietly, his face stained with tears. He looked so abjectly miserable that she wanted to scoop him up in her arms and cuddle him.

The nurse who was with him said softly, 'His name's Josh Hargrove. He scalded himself with hot coffee, and blisters have started to form. His blood pressure is low and his pulse is rapid.'

Sasha nodded. 'Thanks, Megan,' she said, and then turned to the child. 'Hello, Josh,' she said. 'I'm Sasha. I'm a doctor, and I'm going to help Megan to look after you. I'm sorry to hear that you've hurt yourself. Can I have a look at your chest to see what's happened to you? I want to do what I can to make you feel a little more comfortable.'

He was slumped on the bed, clearly going into shock, but he roused himself enough to complain, 'You not touch my poorly.' His mouth jutted.

'It's very sore, is it?'

He nodded, and she said softly, 'I'll be very careful. I just want to see how it looks.' She helped him to lie back against his pillows and then looked searchingly at his injury.

Nathan said in a low voice, 'The skin on his chest is badly inflamed and it's obviously causing him a lot of distress.'

Sasha nodded. She talked to the child quietly for a while, and when he was settled and more confident about letting her treat him, she reached into a box by the bedside and produced a cotton bag. 'Do you want to have a look in there while I take a look at your chest? Be careful, though. I think there's a poorly teddy bear in there. He's hurt himself as well.'

The boy's eyes widened. He felt inside the bag and drew out the small, golden bear, then looked up at Sasha. 'He's got a bandage on him,' he said, a question in his voice.

Sasha nodded. 'He's hurt his chest, just like you. Shall we give him some medicine for the pain? That might make him feel better.'

The boy nodded, and Sasha handed him a small measuring cup. 'Here you are. You can give it to him if you like. The nurse will help you.'

She watched as the boy shakily put the cup to the teddy's lips, and then handed him a cup for himself. 'Will you drink this for me? It will help to make you feel a bit better, too.'

He did as she asked, and she said to Nathan, 'It's quite an extensive burn. I think we'll put him on IV fluids to replace those that he's lost, and he'll need antibiotics to prevent any infection.' To Megan, she said, 'We'll cover the area with a non-stick dressing to keep it moist, and admit him for observation.'

Megan nodded. 'I'll make the arrangements.'

Sasha did her best to reassure the boy and then managed to quickly set up the intravenous line. Once she was satisfied that she had done everything possible for her small patient, she took Megan to one side and said quietly, 'Do we know who brought him in? I thought we were going to let parents come and be with their children?' If Matt had intervened to countermand her request, she would have something to say about it.

Megan grimaced. 'Actually, it was the nanny who brought him here. She was a bit overwrought and she was making him more upset, so Amanda took her off to calm her down.'

'I'm not surprised she was in a state,' Nathan said. 'Apparently she had left her coffee-cup near the edge of a table while she went to answer the phone, and the accident shook her up. At least she had the good sense to keep the boy's chest area clean and covered with a damp cloth, and she brought him here straight away.'

'That's something, anyway. I'll go and have a word with her.'

'You no go,' Josh said, rousing himself as she started to draw the curtain to one side. 'I don't want you to go.' Tears trickled down his face.

Sasha went over to him and gently stroked his hair. 'I shan't be far away,' she murmured. 'I'm just going to find your nanny and tell her that she can come and see you.'

He shook his head. 'Don't want to see Janie. She's horrible. She shouts at me and tells me to go away. I want my mummy. Mummy never tells me go away.' He began to cry all over again, and Sasha tried to soothe him, placing the teddy bear in the crook of his arm.

Beside her, Nathan shifted awkwardly. She glanced up at him, a question in her eyes. He moved away from the bedside and said in a low voice, 'I wondered about the nanny. I spoke to her earlier and I wasn't impressed.' He made a face. 'She's good-looking, though. It crossed my mind that perhaps the father had chosen her to take care of his son, but maybe I'm being uncharitable.'

Sasha grimaced. Turning back to the little boy, she said softly, 'Do you know, teddy wants his mummy as well? He's very unhappy, just like you, but I'm sure you can make him smile again. Can you give him a cuddle?'

The boy dashed away his tears and then curved his arm around the bear and held onto him. He looked up at her. 'Janie took my teddy away,' he said, his mouth beginning to tremble. ''Cos I was naughty.'

'Did she?' Sasha made a sad face. 'How were you naughty?'

His eyes filled up with tears. 'I broke the medicine bottle. I didn't mean to… I was just looking, but she made me jump.'

Sasha hazarded a guess at what might have happened. 'Because she came into the room and saw you with it?'

He nodded. 'I didn't know it was medicine. It was on the table in the kitchen…and she won't give me my teddy back.'

Sasha gave him a gentle hug. 'I'm sorry to hear that. Try not to worry about it now. We need you to rest as much as you can.'

Sasha glanced at Megan. She mouthed softly, 'Do we know where his mother is?'

Megan shook her head. She said in a low voice, 'I

don't know how to contact her, and the nanny wasn't very forthcoming about the background. She kept saying she just wanted us to treat him as soon as possible, so that she could take him home.'

Sasha frowned, and then turned her attention back to the little boy. 'Try not to fret,' she said. 'I'm sure we'll manage to sort everything out for you.'

Josh looked up at her, his grey eyes drenched with tears once again. 'Uncle Matt said he'd find my mummy, but she's not come back.' His voice quavered. 'I want my mummy.'

Uncle Matt? Sasha frowned and a nagging feeling of uncertainty began to creep through her. There had been no mention of a father in all this, and she was beginning to be concerned about what was going on. Was this some awful trick of fate? Who was this little boy, and why weren't his parents hurrying to be here by his side?

She put an arm around the boy's shoulders. 'I know you want your mummy, sweetheart. I need to go and see if I can find out where she is.' She glanced up at Nathan. 'Will you stay with him while I go and make some enquiries?'

'Of course.'

Sasha stroked the child's cheek. 'You can keep this teddy if you like.' It was one she had brought from home, and she could easily replace it.

'Can I?' His mouth opened in wonder, and his eyes brightened.

'Yes, you can.'

He smiled for the first time, and stroked the teddy's fur, and Sasha felt as though the sun had come out.

She said, 'Will you stay here with the doctor and Megan, and look after teddy, while I go and talk to some people? I'll be back in a little while, I promise.'

He nodded, and Sasha slipped away from the cubicle to go in search of Matt. Surely he was back from his meeting? He was probably on a lunch-break by now, but she would look for him anyway. Instinct told her that something was very wrong here.

He was in his office, dictating notes for his secretary, and she knocked on the glass door and went in without giving him time to answer. 'I didn't mean to disturb you,' she said, 'but I have a problem and I wondered if you might be able to help.'

He switched off the machine and looked at her. 'It sounds as though it's urgent. Is it a problem with a patient?'

She nodded. 'A little boy. He was brought in, suffering from a scald to his chest, and I'm having trouble finding his immediate family.'

He frowned. 'Have you tried the welfare agency? Their office is just down the hall. You could give them a ring, or drop in and talk to them.'

'No, I haven't done that yet. I thought I'd try you first. The boy's name is Hargrove. Josh Hargrove. It just occurred to me that he might be a relative of yours.'

Matt looked perplexed, and before Sasha could say any more, he was on his feet and heading towards the door. 'Where is he now? What happened to him?'

'He's still in the treatment bay. I'm arranging for him to be admitted, because the burn covers quite a large area. They're second-degree burns, so hopefully he should come through this without any scarring, but he's shocked and upset, and I think we need to keep an eye on him.'

'Who brought him in?'

'His nanny, Jane Maidstone.' She glanced at him, and saw that his expression was bleak. 'Do you know who he is?'

'I think you've already guessed, haven't you? He's my nephew.'

'I'm so sorry.' It didn't make her feel any better to know that her guess had been accurate. She said hurriedly, 'I do think he'll be all right, but he's upset and asking for his mother.'

Matt's mouth made a grim line. 'I wish I knew where I could find her. She's not in any of the places I might have expected her to be. I've tried all the agencies for missing people but they haven't been able to come up with anything yet. It's as though she's disappeared off the face of the earth.'

Sasha didn't know what to say to him. She murmured cautiously, 'I'm surprised that Jane didn't ask for you. She knows that you work here, doesn't she?'

'I told her that I was going to be in a meeting in a hospital across town for most of the morning. I expect she was waiting until I returned.'

By now, they had reached the treatment bay, and Matt went into the cubicle to look in on the child. Sasha saw Josh's face light up when he saw who had come to visit him. Nathan was checking his chart, but he moved to one side as Matt walked in.

Josh cried out, 'Uncle Matt... You're here... I didn't know you was here.' His face crumpled. 'I burned myself. It hurts...a lot.'

'Poor little man.' Matt sat down beside the boy and lightly tousled his hair. 'Have the doctors and nurses been looking after you?'

Josh nodded solemnly. 'Dr Nathan and Dr Sasha looked after me. I like Dr Sasha. She said she'd come back and see me.'

Sasha gave a faint smile and retreated with Nathan, leaving Matt to talk to his little nephew. The child was solemn, his grey eyes large in his pale face, but he was happy to be with his uncle, and that was heartening.

His outburst when she had mentioned his nanny still bothered her and maybe it would be for the best if she went to have a word with her. The boy was frightened by what had happened to him and his emotions were raw, and that probably accounted for what he had said. The nanny was most likely distraught and craving information.

'I think I ought to go and have a word with the nanny,' Sasha murmured, and Nathan nodded.

'I wonder how near I was to the truth,' he murmured. 'Matt's a single man, and from what I've heard he's left a trail of broken hearts behind him on his travels. He probably has an eye for a pretty face. I can't say I saw much else to recommend the nanny.'

'I didn't hear about any broken hearts,' Sasha muttered.

Nathan's mouth made a crooked slant. 'Oh, yes. The grapevine's been working overtime. He doesn't stay around to pick up the pieces. His job comes first and he moves on when the time comes.'

Sasha grimaced. That was more than she wanted to hear. Were all men so fickle that they couldn't stay and be faithful to one woman? She had already guessed that Matt was ambitious.

She left Nathan with a patient and went in search of the nanny. She found her in the waiting room, pacing the floor like a caged animal. When Sasha entered, the girl turned and hurried towards her.

'Do you have some news for me?' She was an attractive young woman, as Nathan had said, with long blonde hair that shifted restlessly in silken strands over her shoulders as she talked. 'How is he?'

Sasha gave her a swift run-down of what was happening, and the girl frowned. 'Are you certain that he needs to be admitted? It was just his chest. I did what I could to minimise the damage straight away.'

'We need to keep an eye on him for a day or so. He's suffering a little from shock, and the burn is quite nasty. We have to make sure that there's no infection. I know it's upsetting, but you'll be able to see him in a little while.'

Jane grimaced. 'I was hoping that I could take him home before…' She broke off and then added, 'It didn't seem all that bad at the time.' She clasped her arms over her chest in a protective gesture. 'I keep telling him to be careful, but he won't keep away from anything. It doesn't matter what I leave on the table, he's always into it, checking it over, seeing if it's anything he can play with. When he's not poking around with my things, he's climbing up where he shouldn't, and getting into mischief. Only the other day he almost pulled the contents of the Welsh dresser down on him.' She grimaced. 'Now I'm bound to get in trouble, and all because he couldn't leave things alone.'

Sasha frowned. 'As I understand it, he pulled a cup of coffee over himself. Black coffee, that was almost at boiling point.'

'Yes, that's right. He knows I drink it that way.' She made a face. 'No matter how much I tell him, he never learns. I told him I was waiting for a phone call from my friend, and that he had to behave himself.'

Sasha pulled in a deep breath. 'He's only four years old, and most little boys are naturally inquisitive about everything around them. Perhaps you should keep dangerous things well away from him, so as to avoid any risk of him hurting himself.'

'I know. I'll remember next time I make coffee.'

Sasha was beginning to dislike this woman. How on earth had she managed to convince anyone that she was fit to look after a child? What had Matt been thinking of when he'd employed her—or hadn't he been thinking at all? Was Nathan on the right track? Had he been blinded by the girl's looks? Frowning, she dismissed the thought. Matt wouldn't be so foolish, would he?

Sasha said coolly, 'Would you like to go and see Josh?' It was beginning to occur to her that the nanny's remarks might have sounded more callous than she had intended. To be fair to her, the girl was probably upset about what had happened, and stressed out, and she ought to give her the benefit of the doubt. 'We could arrange for you to stay with him overnight, if you like. He'll be feeling insecure and having someone familiar close by might help.'

She couldn't be certain that Josh's remarks hadn't been made as a reaction to what had happened to him. If Jane had shouted a warning, he might still be anxious that he had done something wrong.

Jane shook her head. 'I'll go and see him, but I can't stay. I've already made arrangements to go out this evening.'

'As you please.' Sasha stiffened her shoulders. 'I'll ask the nurse to come and tell you when you can go to him. Make yourself comfortable in the meantime.'

She went back to the treatment bay. Matt was still sitting with Josh, and they were looking at a picture-book together. Matt's arm was around the boy and they looked comfortable, as though they were happy to be together.

Sasha stood very still, watching them for a moment. She had never seen Matt like this, tender, smiling, joking with the little boy. He was relaxed, gentle, and she was seeing a completely different side to the man. He was good with his young patients, of course, but this was different. She could see that there was a bond between the two of them.

A lump came into her throat. They looked so at ease with each other, and she was glad that at least Josh had someone who cared about him. Poor little scrap. It must be terrible to be in his situation, to be missing his mum, and not understanding what was going on around him.

She knew that feeling all too well. She had been just a young child when her mother had first been taken ill and admitted to hospital, and she remembered the torrent of loneliness and despair that had swamped her back then. No one had explained to her what was going on, and she had wondered if she would ever see her mother again. Her father had simply retreated into a world of his own. Her brother had been only five or six years old at the time, and his world had been devastated. She had done her best to comfort him, to reassure him that he wasn't alone.

'Thank you for taking care of Josh.' Matt's deep voice intruded on her thoughts and she blinked, her gaze swivelling to him.

'I'm glad that I was able to help him.' She looked at the child. 'How are you feeling now?'

'It doesn't hurt as much,' he said bravely. 'You gave me some medicine, didn't you?'

'That's right.'

Matt spoke quietly to Josh, and told him that he would be back to look in on him in a while. 'Megan will take care of you. I expect she has some more books for you to look at.' The boy nodded cautiously, seeming to accept that but not happy about it.

Matt walked with Sasha away from the treatment

bay. 'I'm glad you thought to come and find me. Josh has had enough to cope with just lately, and it would have been much worse if I hadn't been there for him.'

'It must be difficult for you, not knowing where your sister is, and having to take on his care.'

He gave a faint shrug. 'I'm all he has, and I took him in straight away to live with me, but there isn't too much that I can do for him.'

'So you arranged for a nanny to move in?'

He shrugged. 'I have a job of work to do, and I had to arrange for someone to watch over him when he wasn't at school. Jane's been very good with him, and I've had to leave her to cope with all the everyday problems that crop up.' He frowned. 'I don't know how this could have happened. She's always ultra-careful.'

'Are you certain of that? How did he manage to spill coffee over himself? Can you be sure that there haven't been other similar incidents, near misses?'

He shook his head. 'Why are you so intent on looking for problems where they don't exist? Jane seems totally efficient at what she does, and she's always been very caring towards him.'

Sasha sent him a sceptical look. Had he been completely bowled over by Jane's looks to the extent that he wasn't seeing past the end of his nose? Were men really so easy to manipulate?

Matt's brows met in a dark line. 'What was that look supposed to mean? I can't imagine why you're so convinced that something's wrong,' he said tersely. 'You don't know Jane, or Josh, and yet you appear to have formed an opinion that he isn't being cared for properly. I admit the coffee spill was dangerous, but accidents do happen.'

'Yes, they do, but I'm still not reassured in this case, and as I'm the doctor who is responsible for Josh's well-being just now, I have to admit that I'm concerned. I wouldn't be doing my job properly if I didn't point out my worries on that score.'

'Jane's references were excellent, and I've had no cause for complaint.'

'Until now.' Maybe Jane put on a convincing act around Matt and made it seem as though she was the perfect person to take care of the little boy. Sasha threw him a warning look. 'I'd have a chat with Josh, if I were you, and find out what he really thinks. You're probably in for a surprise.'

'I'll do that,' Matt retorted. 'In the meantime, since you're so wise and all-seeing, perhaps you'd care to look in on our other traumatised young patients. I expect you can sort out their problems, too.'

She gave a tight smile. How was it that he managed to turn the tables and put her in her place with such ease?

She went back to work and tried to put the morning's events to the back of her mind. In her lunch-break, she checked with Theresa that all was well at home, and discovered that the doctor still hadn't made her house call.

'I've had a word with the receptionist at the health centre,' Theresa said, 'and she told me that the doctor was running late. She'd had to deal with an emergency. I'll let you know as soon as I have any news.'

'Thanks, Theresa. Is my mother feeling any better?'

'She's about the same…still coughing and it hurts her to breathe. I think you're right—it does sound like a chest infection. Try not to worry yourself, though. I promise I'll keep an eye on her.'

'You're an angel. How is the studying coming along with all this? Are you managing to get something done?'

'It's hard. I've never been brilliant at academic work, but I really want to get a good grade.' Theresa sighed. 'I've always hoped to have a career as a hospital technician, but I didn't imagine the work would be this hard.'

'Have you thought of asking Sam for help? You're both at the same university, aren't you? And from what I hear, my brother has the same worries as you. Maybe you could help each other.'

'I'm not sure about that. I did try to talk to Sam, but he's having problems of his own. With missing some of the lectures, he's had a lot of catching up to do.'

Sasha was puzzled. 'I didn't know he'd missed any lectures.'

Theresa sucked in a quick breath. 'Oh, I'm sorry… I thought he'd said something to you about it…' Theresa appeared to flounder. 'I expect I have everything back to front as usual. Forget I mentioned it. I'm always getting things wrong.'

'I doubt that. You always seem very level-headed

to me.' Sasha hesitated. She didn't want to make Theresa feel bad about letting the cat out of the bag. 'Sam's determined on becoming a pharmacist, and I don't think he would do anything to jeopardise his chances. I'm sure he knows what he's doing. Don't fret about it.'

Sasha rang off a moment or two later. Theresa's slip of the tongue was bothering her. Why had Sam missed lectures? That wasn't like him at all. She hurried towards the cafeteria. There was just time for her to have a quick meal before she was due back in the emergency room. Perhaps lunch would help her to sift through her worries.

A short time later, she was back at work. Matt saw her frowning as she stood by the desk, studying charts. 'Is there a problem?' he asked. 'Do you need some help?'

'No, thank you,' she murmured. 'I'm just checking some results from the lab. They seem to be fine.'

'Then why the frown?' He was looking at her searchingly.

'It's nothing to do with work,' she answered vaguely. She glanced up at him. Clearly that answer didn't satisfy him. She grimaced. 'Before you say anything, yes, I know that I should be concentrating on what I'm doing and not thinking about other things. I will do my job properly, you don't need to worry about that.'

'There's no need for you to be so defensive. I wasn't going say anything. I'm just concerned for you—you helped me with Josh this morning, and I feel that I owe you.'

Sasha shook her head. 'You don't owe me anything, I was just doing my job, though I have to admit he touched a chord with me. He's so small and vulnerable.'

Matt smiled. 'That's true. He gets to me that way, too.' He studied her. 'So, what's the problem? Is it something to do with home?'

He wasn't going to give up, was he? She sighed, and pushed the chart she was reading back into its slot before turning to face him properly. 'If you must know, my mother isn't too well just at the moment. I'm waiting to hear that the doctor has called.' She couldn't see much point in telling him about her worries over Sam.

He frowned. 'Is it serious? Do you need to take time off to be with her?'

'I think it's a chest infection, perhaps pleurisy even, but someone is looking after her, and if she takes a turn for the worse then, yes, I'll go home.'

'I think I heard on the grapevine that you had moved down here because of your mother. Is that right?'

She nodded, surprised. 'It doesn't take long for things to get around, does it? My mother has never been very strong, so the move was something I'd had in mind for a long time.'

'What was wrong with her? To bring about the move, I mean.' He shot her an apologetic look. 'I hope you don't mind me asking?'

'No. That's all right.' She grimaced again. 'When I was very young, she learned that she had a brain tumour—a pituitary tumour. Sadly, it took quite a while for the doctors to work out exactly what the problem was. She was lucky in that it was benign, but it caused all sorts of problems, and she needed ongoing treatment.'

'These tumours can sometimes be shrunk by radiation therapy or even by medication—is that what happened in your mother's case?'

'Yes, but the treatment wasn't too successful. In the end, the doctors decided that removing it was the only thing to do, and she has had to have replacement therapy ever since to compensate for the lack of production of hormones. She's had all sorts of problems over the years, and I can't help but worry about her. I thought the country air where we live now might help, and visits to the seaside would be easier. I thought they might cheer her up.'

Matt was frowning. 'It's understandable that you would be concerned for her. You must let me know if things get too much for you. If you need time to be at home with her, I'm sure we can arrange something.'

'Thank you.' She sent him a thoughtful glance. 'If you need any help with Josh, once he's back home with you, I'll be glad to do whatever I can. He's a lovely boy. It can't be easy for you, especially with all the worry over your sister, and he must be missing his mother.'

Without thinking, she reached out and touched his

arm. 'I mean it—if there is anything at all that I can do, you only have to ask.'

He glanced down at her hand as it rested lightly on his jacket sleeve. 'Thanks. I appreciate the offer, but he's my responsibility now. There's no need for you to get involved. I'll manage.' He picked up a chart and moved away from the desk and Sasha let her hand fall to her side.

She watched him go. He was straight-backed, moving purposefully towards the treatment bay, alone, self-sufficient, and it worried her that he was so determined to carry everything on his own shoulders.

Why wouldn't he let her lend a hand? It was awful to think of Josh, abandoned, lonely and crying out for help. Was Matt too proud to accept her help?

Or perhaps the truth was simpler than that. He had looked at her hand as it had rested on his arm, and his expression had been closed to her. Was he afraid that she was being too familiar with him?

He was a complex individual without a doubt. He was the boss, and she was just a lowly doctor, and to make matters worse, she was a woman who couldn't keep her opinions to herself. Now she was threatening to interfere in his private life. Did he think that she wanted more from him?

He needn't have worried. She couldn't deny that she was drawn to him, but she didn't want to invade his space or put pressure on him. That wasn't what she had in mind at all.

Hadn't she learned a long time ago that if you put your trust in people, you could get hurt? Her own father had taught her that. He had been selfish, and his children had been the last of his concerns.

She had discovered that relationships could be fickle, and she was wary of getting involved with anyone.

CHAPTER FOUR

'How does that feel, Mum?' Sasha plumped up her mother's pillows and eased her gently back against them. 'Is that any better? It should help your breathing if you can sit up a little.'

'That's perfect, thank you.' Her mother looked at her, her blue eyes troubled. 'I'm sorry that you're having to do all this for me.' Her voice was thready as she tried to speak against the wheeze of her chest. 'I thought I was doing so well, and I don't understand why I'm having this setback.'

'I think perhaps you overdid things as soon as we moved in here. It took more out of you than you expected and left you vulnerable to infection.' Sasha lightly touched her mother's arm. 'I don't want you to worry about anything. Just get as much rest as you can, and let the antibiotics do their work. Remember what the doctor said—you need to take things easy. I can deal with everything that needs to be done.'

'I had such hopes when we moved here. I thought things would work out for us.'

'They will. Once you're over this nasty infection, you'll see—things will be much brighter. With the good weather and all the fresh air, you'll start to feel stronger every day, I'm sure.'

69

'Bless you.' Her mother smiled. 'You're a good girl…you always have been.'

Sasha gave her an answering smile as she handed her a glass of water. 'Here, take your tablets and then try to get some sleep. I'm going to sort through a few chores before I go to work, and Theresa will be here in a while to make sure that you're all right. Just remember that I'll only be a phone call away if you need me.'

'I'll be fine. You get yourself off to work.'

When Sasha left the bedroom, her mother was already drifting off to sleep. That was good. It was what she needed to help her recovery. She only hoped the antibiotics would do the trick.

She left Theresa with instructions about her mother's medication, and then set off for the hospital. She had promised Josh that she would go to see him and there would just be time to look in on him before she had to start work. She wanted to satisfy herself that the little boy was doing all right.

He was in bed on the children's ward, trying to fit the pieces of a colourful jigsaw puzzle together when Sasha arrived. 'Uncle Matt bringed it for me,' he said, and confided happily, 'And the nurses gave me a colouring book and some pencils.'

'You're a lucky boy, aren't you?' She saw that the drip was still in place in his arm, and surreptitiously checked his dressing. It looked OK, but she knew it would take some time for the wound to heal.

'How's teddy doing?' she asked him. 'Is his chest getting better?'

Josh shook his head, looking serious. 'It hurts him a lot—it stings.' His mouth made a straight line. 'He'll be all right. I'm looking after him. He likes me to look after him.'

'I'm sure he does.' Sasha sat down beside him and looked at the jigsaw puzzle. 'Are you struggling with this bit? Shall we try to do it together?'

Josh's face brightened. Sasha helped him to put a couple of pieces in place, and then turned around as she heard a noise behind her.

'Hello. What are you doing here?' Matt was holding a towel as he entered the room from a side door. He stopped, and stared at her, running his glance over her slender figure, his gaze travelling over the smoothly fitting cotton top she was wearing and her narrow skirt, before returning to linger on the bright mass of her hair.

'I just thought I'd drop by to see how Josh was doing.' She stared at him, her mouth going dry, the breath catching in her throat.

He was wearing dark trousers that moulded themselves to his hips, and he had on a fresh linen shirt that was still unbuttoned at the throat. She couldn't help but note that he was flat-stomached and perfectly proportioned. His hair was damp, gleaming with iridescent lights as though he had just showered.

He must have picked up on her confusion, because he said shortly, 'I stayed here overnight, so that I could be with Josh. I've just been to the washroom to clean up.'

'Oh, I see.' She swallowed. She hadn't seen him

like this before, his shirtsleeves rolled back to reveal lightly bronzed forearms, his hair still faintly tousled.

He started to straighten his sleeves, buttoning the cuffs, and then picked up his jacket from the back of a chair. He gave her an intent look, his eyes narrowed. 'Aren't you supposed to be on duty this morning?'

'Yes, but I wanted to come here first.' She got to her feet and started to back away, disturbed by that unswerving grey gaze. 'I'm not late. There's another quarter of an hour before my shift starts.'

Josh said eagerly, 'She's been helping me with the puzzle.'

She smiled at him. 'You've done well to manage so much of it by yourself, Josh.'

Matt said, 'Are you this concerned about all of your patients?'

She sent him a wary look, and his dark brows were expressive. She said in an undertone, 'I'm conscious that I need to do my best for all of them, of course, but in this case Josh asked me if I would come and see him and I didn't want to let him down.' She hesitated. Luckily, Josh was engrossed in his puzzle once more and wasn't paying them much attention.

'I didn't think there would be a problem in my dropping by.' How could she tell him that she felt a strange affinity to Josh, and that she felt deeply about his plight? It touched a chord with her, but Matt wouldn't understand and it was beyond her to explain.

She said awkwardly, 'I should go now. I have to get ready for work.'

He watched as she said goodbye to Josh, and she felt his gaze burn into her as she left the room.

Down in A and E, she was plunged straight into work, and by lunchtime she was feeling the pressure. A little girl was brought in by ambulance, and Sasha quickly went to examine her.

'Hello, Kimberley,' she greeted her. 'Can you hear me? Can you tell me what happened?'

The little girl was unresponsive. She was about six years old, and the paramedic reported that she had been stung by a bee.

'We've managed to remove the sting, but she had already suffered a bad reaction,' he said. 'We've given her an injection of adrenaline, but it hasn't done the trick.'

A woman came rushing in, and Megan told Sasha quietly, 'This is the child's mother.'

'What's happening to her?' the woman said, her voice rising. 'Why is my little girl like this? Why isn't she talking?'

'The venom in the sting has caused a nasty reaction,' Sasha told her. 'It's causing inflammation which is affecting Kimberley and causing her tissues to swell.'

'But it was just one sting,' the woman cried, her tone verging on hysteria. 'This can't be happening.'

Sasha was conscious that Matt had come to see what was going on, and she guessed the noise must have alerted him. It didn't bother her that he was observing, but she was worried that he would remove the mother from the room.

'I'm sorry. We're doing what we can for her, and I hope you can be patient for a while and let us do our jobs. I need to work with her now.' Sasha turned her attention to the child and had to shift position as the woman intruded.

Megan tried to calm the woman, drawing her away, while Sasha continued to examine the little girl. Sasha heard her explaining what was going on, but the woman didn't appear to be listening. She was trying to push her way forward, again, trying to be close to her child.

'I'm going to have to intubate,' Sasha said. Amanda was assisting, and Sasha was glad that she was around. She was competent, used to dealing with this kind of problem.

'There's already a lot of swelling, and it's going to be difficult, but we need to get her on oxygen right away.' As soon as the tube was in place, Sasha put in an IV line and started to give the child more adrenaline.

The mother edged her way forward. 'Why is that tube down her throat? Is it bad? She looks awful. Her lips are swollen. Why is she wheezing like that?'

Sasha said quietly to Amanda, 'Let's raise the child's legs. That should help to improve the blood flow to the heart and brain.'

To the mother, she said, 'The tube is there to help her to breathe. She's wheezing because her chest is tight and so I'm going to give her medication along with the oxygen to try to improve the situation. The salbutamol will help to widen her airways.'

The child's condition didn't appear to be improving, and the mother was becoming more and more agitated as time went by. Sasha turned to her.

'As I said before, Kimberley has suffered a nasty reaction to the bee sting. We're doing everything we can to put things right. What I need you to do is to remain very calm, and hold your daughter's hand. You need to be quiet, for her, and do what you can to soothe her gently.'

'But she looks so ill,' the mother said, her voice high-pitched. 'You have to do something, quickly.'

Matt's gaze went from the child to the mother. 'We are doing everything possible,' he told her in a low voice, 'but it isn't going to help your little girl if you keep on showing your distress in this way. It will only make her more frightened, and that will make her condition worse. You must calm down.'

The woman sobered. 'I'm sorry,' she said. 'It's so upsetting to see her like this.'

'If it bothers you,' he murmured, 'the nurse will take you into the waiting room.'

The woman shook her head. 'No, I want stay with her. Please, let me stay.'

Amanda said suddenly, 'The child isn't breathing. There's no pulse.'

Sasha acted swiftly. She began to give cardiac compressions to start the heart. 'We need more adrenaline,' she said, and breathed a sigh of relief when the child's pulse returned. 'Let's get some fluids into her, and we'll try an antihistamine and steroids.'

After some time, the child began to respond to the

treatment, and Sasha breathed a sigh of relief. She left her in the care of Amanda and Megan, while she took the mother to one side.

'We've managed to stabilise Kimberley's condition, and I'm hopeful that she will come through this all right. What you need to know is that this reaction could happen again if she was to be stung at another time. I'm going to ask the nurse to show you how to deal with that situation, should it happen. We'll also arrange for Kimberley to be seen on an outpatient basis, so that we can monitor her. It may be that we can give her a course of desensitising injections, but that will be for the specialist to decide.' She paused. 'Don't worry if you haven't understood everything. I've said. I'll ask the nurse to go through it with you again.'

'Thank you,' the woman said. 'I'm really grateful for what you've done. I'm so sorry that I was hysterical. I was so frightened.'

'That's all right. It's understandable that you were upset. You managed to calm yourself down in the end, and that's what's important.'

Sasha went back to her patient and made sure that all was well. Megan took the mother away to explain what needed to happen next, and Sasha went to the desk to write up her notes. Matt had watched everything, and she had no idea how he would react. Was he going to say that parents couldn't be present when their child was treated? Things had not gone well this morning.

She looked up as he approached. His expression

was sober, and she wondered if that was bad news. 'The little girl seems to be doing well now,' she said.

'Yes, she does.' He looked at her steadily. 'It was a difficult situation for you, with the mother creating such a disturbance.'

Sasha gave him a wary look. 'It can't have been easy for her. No one wants to see her child in that situation. It's very frightening.'

'That's true, but having a parent behave in that way can cause distress to the child, and it can make treating the patient much harder.'

Sasha frowned. 'I know that, but I still think that it's better for parents and children to be together. In the right circumstances it can be helpful for the child.' She looked at him guardedly from under her lashes. 'I hope you're not thinking of going to go back to the old system. I know I didn't handle it too well today. I was concentrating on dealing with the child, and there wasn't time for me to talk to the parent, but instinctively I still feel that it's the right thing to do.'

'The policy was put in place by the consultant who was here before me. We haven't seen any need to change it up to now.'

Her brows drew together. 'Some children are very upset when they are separated from their parents.'

He nodded. 'Yes, I realise that, but we have to be able to get on and treat them without hindrance. What went on just then wasn't helpful. It could have been handled better.'

She bit her lip. 'I know that… I know I should have done more to soothe the mother and prevent problems, but we can make it work, I'm sure.' Sasha looked at him anxiously. Was he planning on putting an end to what she had started without giving her a chance?

'Perhaps.' He didn't sound convinced. 'When you're the doctor in charge, you have to concentrate on doing the best for your patient, and any distraction is going to make things more difficult, especially when you're under pressure. I suggest that you draw up some guidelines for how you think we should handle the situation when parents are present. We need to know how we are going to react if a parent starts to cause problems. If you can outline our options in various instances, then we'll all be working from the same sheet.'

She stared at him. 'Does that mean you're going to do things my way?' She had hardly dared imagine that after this morning's problem he would give it any more consideration.

'I'm making no promises. I'm saying that we'll give it a try, and to do that properly we need to be clear as to how we're going to deal with certain situations. Perhaps you can draw up a course of action?'

She wanted fling her arms round him and kiss him. Her eyes widened. 'That's wonderful—yes, of course I'll do that.' Her smile was wide. 'Thanks, Matt.'

His mouth twisted. 'Don't get too carried away. I'm not persuaded that this will be practicable. I haven't said that we'll implement it yet, only that we'll give it a go. Let's just see if we can make it work.'

Sasha was determined to make it work. Over the next few days she set up a plan of action and talked everyone through it. Maybe having Matt as a boss wasn't going to be nearly as bad as she had thought. He was at least open to new ideas.

A few days later, Sasha was working with a patient when she saw Matt go to greet someone. The man was around sixty years old, and his hair, though once black, was now greying. His eyes were dark, and Sasha was struck by the resemblance between him and Matt. Was this Matt's father?

'Hi, Dad. What are you doing here?' Matt was smiling, bringing the man into the room.

So she had guessed right. Sasha watched them as she finished suturing her patient's wound. Josh was with the man. He had been discharged from hospital the day before yesterday, and his chest was healing nicely by all accounts. The little boy looked around the department, his gaze wondering, trying to take it all in.

'Where's Sasha?' he asked. He moved away from his grandfather's side and started to wander about the room.

Sasha handed her patient over to a nurse and left the treatment bay to go and see the little boy. 'Hello, Josh,' she said. 'How are you? Are you feeling better?'

He nodded. 'I was looking for you.'

'I know. I was over there, and you couldn't see me, but I saw you.' It wasn't a good idea for him to be wandering about the department, and obviously Matt and his father thought so, too, because they came after him.

'Sorry about that,' the older man said. 'I only took my eyes off him for a second.'

'That's all right. I'm glad to see him looking so well. He had a nasty burn, but from all accounts it's much better now.'

'It is.' The man looked at her. 'You must be Sasha. Josh has been telling me all about you.' His mouth curved. 'I'm William Benton, Matt's father.' He held out his hand to her. 'I'm pleased to meet you, Sasha. You did a good job with Josh.'

She extended her own hand and he clasped it warmly, saying, 'I've just come here to talk to Matt about the boy's mother.' He grimaced. 'It's a difficult time for all of us, as I expect you know.'

Sasha said quietly, 'I'm sure it must be. Would you like me to look after Josh while you have a chat? I'm on a break now, so it's no trouble.'

'Would you? Thanks. That would be a great help.'

Matt was frowning, but William handed Josh over and turned away to his son. 'I had a phone call from Helen,' Sasha heard him say. 'She wouldn't tell me where she was, but it's obvious that she wanted to know how Josh was doing. That's something at least, isn't it? I just wish we had some idea of how to find her. I'm getting more worried by the day.'

Sasha didn't catch Matt's muttered reply. Putting on a bright face, she looked down at Josh and said, 'Shall we go into the doctors' lounge for a little while? I might be able to find a glass of milk for you, and some biscuits.' She saw that he was clutching his teddy bear. 'I expect teddy will want a biscuit,' she said. 'Is his chest better now?'

Josh chatted to her eagerly, telling her about his day, and how his grandad had let him sit in his big leather chair in his surgery. 'He looks after people who is poorly,' he said, 'but he doesn't work all the time…just sometimes. He's looking after me now.'

'Is he?'

'Yes, but I'm staying at Uncle Matt's house. He gives me chocolate. Mummy doesn't let me have chocolate much, but Uncle Matt does.' He smiled like a conspirator. 'He says we won't tell.'

Sasha smiled with him. 'You're doing all right, then, aren't you?'

'Yes.' He paused, then said solemnly, 'But Mummy's gone away. I want Mummy.' He looked dejected.

'I know you do, sweetheart. I'm sure your uncle Matt and your grandad are doing what they can to find her.'

He nodded doubtfully and she distracted him with cookies and a pen and paper. 'Do you want to draw a picture? I think Uncle Matt and Grandad will like that.'

He sat down at the table and began to draw. The tip of his tongue peeped out as he concentrated, and Sasha watched him while she made herself a cup of coffee. When he had finished, he showed her his picture and said excitedly, 'It's a house…Uncle Matt's house. There's a chimney, look, and there's trees in the garden. He don't have a swing for me to play on like Mummy does.'

Sasha looked at the drawing. 'It's lovely,' she said. There was a crooked house with a twisted triangle for a roof, hovering precariously on a wobbly line. In the garden there were what looked like lollipops, and she guessed they were trees.

Matt came in as she was admiring the picture. He glanced at Sasha. 'Is everything all right in here? Sorry to have left you for so long.'

'That's all right. We've been fine.'

Josh clutched his drawing and went off happily to greet Matt, tugging fiercely at his jacket so that he could show him what he had done.

'Look, Uncle Matt. See what I've done.' He pulled at Matt's belt, eager for his attention.

'That's my house?' Matt said, twisting around a little to face him properly, and looking down at the paper. 'I hadn't realised it looked like that. It's very good, isn't it?' He smiled at the child. 'It's time to go now, Josh,' he said. 'Say goodbye to Sasha. Grandad's ready to take you home.'

Matt glanced up and nodded to Sasha. 'Thanks for keeping an eye on him.'

'I was happy to do it.'

He went out with the boy, and Sasha went over to the sink to wash out her coffee-cup before going back to work. It was only later, when she was getting ready to go home, and she went back to the lounge to collect her jacket, that she discovered Josh had left his teddy bear behind. It was on a chair beneath the coat rack.

She bent to pick it up and discovered beside it a small wallet, very much like a credit-card case.

She examined it cautiously. From the contents, she could see that it belonged to Matt. Had it dropped from his pocket when Josh had tugged at his jacket earlier? Perhaps it had been in his trouser pocket and had become dislodged. She frowned. Either way, surely he would be missing it? She went to look for him.

'He left some time ago,' Amanda said. 'He had a meeting with management, and then he said he was going to pick up Josh from his dad's house. I expect he'll be home any time now.'

'Do you know where he lives, or his home phone number? I found something that belongs to him, and I guess that he'll be missing it before too long.' There could be a problem if he was planning an evening out or wanted to buy petrol or something and discovered that his credit card was gone. Josh, too, would probably be feeling sad to lose his teddy. She didn't like to think of the child fretting when he was being tucked up in bed that night.

'He has a house in the same village as you,' Amanda said. 'I'm surprised you haven't bumped into each other before now. The desk clerk will have the address, but I think he lives at Brookside, near the park.'

'That's a nice area,' Sasha commented. 'The houses are all very impressive and exclusive. A bit too pricey for me, I'm afraid. I'm on the opposite side of the park where the lesser mortals live.' She made a face and Amanda chuckled.

'There's time yet. You only have to make the consultant grade.'

Sasha's eyes lifted heavenward. 'As if.'

Since it turned out that she lived reasonably close to Matt, it wouldn't be too much trouble to return the card case and the teddy, would it, rather than have Matt come all the way back to the hospital for them?

She set off for home just a short time later. Brookside was just a short distance from where she lived, and she could leave the car at her house and take a short cut across the park to find them and drop the things off. It would be quicker that way and the fresh air would do her good.

She checked with Theresa first. 'It's all right,' the girl said. 'You go ahead. Your mother's asleep. I'm all right to stay on for a while.'

'Thanks. I'll try not to be too long.'

As it happened, she caught sight of Josh and Matt walking across the grass, by the brook that meandered through the park.

'Matt,' she called. 'Josh…wait…'

They both turned and looked towards her. Josh jumped up and down excitedly, ready to run towards her, but Matt held onto his hand. They started in her direction, and when they met up, Matt looked at her quizzically.

'Sasha? This is unexpected. Don't tell me you live around here, too?'

'I do,' she said. 'I live in the little cul-de-sac at the

back of the sports field. It's a small world, isn't it?' She smiled at Josh and then looked back at Matt. 'I'm glad that I managed to catch up with you. I found this in the doctors' lounge.' She handed over the card case. 'I think it must have dropped out of your pocket and I was worried that you might need it.'

Matt stared at the leather wallet, looking bemused, and she added, 'I found this, too.' She passed the teddy to Josh and the little boy clutched it to him.

His eyes shone. 'I thought I lost him. I was crying.'

'He was on a chair at the hospital,' Sasha murmured. 'I felt sure that you would be missing him.'

Matt frowned. 'Thanks for bringing these over to us,' he said. 'You're right, I'll need this later on, and I would have been wondering what had happened to it. I can't think how I came to lose it.'

'I imagine it fell from your pocket when Josh was showing you his drawing.'

He nodded. 'That could account for it.' He looked down at Josh and the frown was back. 'I thought you had a teddy bear at home.'

'Janie took him.' Josh's mouth wavered. 'She didn't give him back.'

Matt's brows drew together. 'I'll look for him. He might be in a cupboard somewhere.'

Sasha murmured, 'Can't you ask Jane where she put him?'

'If I can't find the teddy I'll give her a ring. She's not with us any more.'

Sasha's eyes widened. 'Isn't she?'

He shook his head. 'Josh didn't like her, so my

father and I are managing the best we can, along with a neighbour who helps out.'

Had he discovered that Jane was not what she seemed? She didn't like to question him further. 'It sounds as though things are difficult for you.'

He shrugged. 'It isn't the best of situations, but so far things are working out reasonably well.'

'I'm glad.' She sent him a quick sideways glance. 'You know, I meant what I said the other day...if I can help at all, you only have to say.'

'It's good of you to offer, but I'm sure we'll manage.' He gave her a smile. 'Are you setting off for home now? I expect you'll be glad of a break. We've had a busy day.'

'They're all busy. I sometimes think we could do with twice the staff to spread the load.'

'You have a point there.'

Josh tugged at Sasha's skirt. 'Are you going home? Can I come to your house?' His eyes lit up. 'Today?'

Matt was quick to nip that in the bud. He frowned. 'Sasha's busy, Josh, and we have things to do back home.'

The boy looked crestfallen, and Sasha winced. It was no trouble to her if the child wanted to visit, and she was sad to see him unhappy. He had already lost his mother and although she couldn't do anything about that, she could at least try to smooth his path.

Matt seemed determined to cope on his own, though. Was it a matter of male pride? Perhaps he didn't feel that it was right to put his problems onto other people.

She said softly, 'I live just across the way. Perhaps a cup of tea wouldn't be out of order? I could show you the revisions I've made to the guidelines about dealing with relatives. I've been putting the finishing touches to them at home, changing things that haven't worked out and finding alternatives. Things have been pretty hectic at work lately, and I haven't been able to go through them with you.'

Matt gave her a steady look, and she guessed he knew it was a less than subtle way of appeasing Josh. 'I suppose this would be a good opportunity,' he said. 'I think we could manage a few minutes.' He looked down at Josh. 'We'll go to Sasha's house—but just for a little while, mind.'

Josh's smile was wide as they headed back across the park. He was hopping and skipping and eager to get there.

Theresa wasn't in the kitchen when they arrived at the house, and from the sounds of movement overhead Sasha guessed she was upstairs, checking on her mother. 'Hi, Mum…Theresa,' she called. 'I'm home. I'll make us a drink.' She filled the kettle and switched it on.

'I'll go up and see her in a minute,' she told Matt. 'I expect Theresa's helping her to the bathroom if she's just woken up.'

Turning to Josh, she said, 'There's a swing in my garden. Would you like to try it out?'

He nodded eagerly and she took him through the kitchen and out into the enclosed garden.

'That's unusual,' Matt commented, standing alongside her and surveying the lawn and neat flower-beds. 'I wouldn't have expected you to have a play area out here. When you're married, with children of your own perhaps, but not just yet. Or is there something you haven't told me?' He made a wry smile, sending her a quizzical look.

'The previous owners left the equipment behind,' she explained. 'Their children had grown up and they asked us to get rid of them. We didn't, though. We decided to hang onto them, in case we had any young visitors who might enjoy them.'

Josh was having a great time on the swing. 'There's a little wheelbarrow, about your size,' she told him. 'It's just right for moving things about, and you can have a go with it, if you like. There are some old plant pots that need to be moved to the table out there. Would you like to do that, while I go and get us something to eat and drink?'

He nodded vigorously. 'I like your garden.'

'I'm glad. Come back to the house when you've finished playing out here.' She turned to Matt. 'We can watch him from the kitchen, if that's all right with you,' she said. 'I want to make a snack for my mother.'

'That's OK.' He went with her back to the house. 'How long have you lived here?'

'Not long. About three months. There's still a lot to do to get the place how we want it, but we made a start on the kitchen and the living room first of all.' She filled the kettle and set out cups and a plate for biscuits and sponge fingers while he glanced around the kitchen.

'It looks good. I like the colour scheme.'

She doubted it would compare well with anything that he had, but she was pleased with it. The walls were a soft yellow, the colour of sunshine, and the cupboards were a complementary pale oak. There were bright touches in the window blind and the tiles, and Sasha had added the odd vase and containers that caught the eye in an agreeable way.

'I'm happy with it.' She frowned. 'My mother helped with some of the decoration and tried to deal with the flower borders outside, but it was all too much for her. I think that's why she's ill now.'

'Do you want to go and look in on her? I'll watch Josh.'

'Thanks, yes, I would. Sit down at the table and help yourself to tea and cake.' She pushed a cup and plate towards him. 'There's milk for Josh. I'll just get those guidelines for you. They're in a folder that I keep specially for work stuff.' She fished them out from an overhead cupboard and handed the papers to him. 'I won't be more than a minute. I'll just find out where Theresa has got to.'

She hurried upstairs, and saw that Theresa was helping her mother back into bed. Her mother looked frail and very ill, much worse than she had been that morning. Sasha rushed over to the bedside.

'Mum, what's wrong? Has something happened? Have you been taking the tablets the doctor prescribed for you?'

'Yes, I have. Don't worry,' her mother managed, fighting to get her breath. 'I'll be all right in a minute or two. I don't mean to be a bother.'

Theresa was looking worried. 'I don't understand how this can have come on so suddenly. I checked just a short time ago, but she was sleeping and she seemed to be all right.'

'It isn't your fault, Theresa,' Sasha said. 'You did what you could.' She put an arm around her mother's shoulders. 'Let me lift you up a bit. That might help. Lying down has probably made your chest clog up a bit.'

'She said her chest hurts,' Theresa said, 'and she's very hot to the touch.'

Sasha put a hand to her mother's forehead. 'You're burning up, Mum,' she said quietly. 'I'm going to give you some paracetamol. That will help relieve the pain and bring down your temperature. Then I'll give the GP a call. I don't think your antibiotics are working very well, and you may need a different kind.'

Her mother didn't argue, and that showed Sasha how bad she must be feeling.

Turning to Theresa, she said, 'I'm going to get my emergency bag. I think she needs to have oxygen to help her breathing, and as soon as I've organised that, I'm going to call the doctor.'

A minute or two later, Sasha had made sure that her mother was breathing through an oxygen mask and she applied regular pressure to the ventilation bag.

'I'll see to that,' Theresa said. 'You go and make your phone call.'

'Are you sure you can manage?'

Theresa nodded. 'I'll be fine.'

'Thanks. Give me a shout if you need me.' Sasha made sure that her mother was in no immediate danger, then left her with Theresa and hurried downstairs to use the phone. The doctor promised to call in on her evening rounds.

'Can I help?' Matt said, coming into the hall. 'Has your mother taken a turn for the worse?'

'I think it's pneumonia,' Sasha told him. 'She looks terrible, and I'm pretty sure that she'll have to go to hospital. I've made her as comfortable as I can for the moment.' She sent him a quick look. 'Is Josh all right?'

'He's eating cake and drinking a glass of milk, and trying to get teddy to do the same. He's fine.'

The doorbell rang just then, and Sasha wondered what else could go wrong today. She hurried to answer it, and found her brother Sam on the doorstep.

'Lost my key,' he said. 'It's probably at the bottom of my holdall. I thought I'd come home for a day or so, and do some work for the exams. It's just revision. There aren't any more lectures, just tutorial groups.'

She stared at him. 'Sam, you look awful. Haven't you been sleeping?'

There were dark shadows under his eyes, and his brown hair stuck up in spikes. He mumbled a reply and then dumped a canvas bag on the hall floor. 'Pile of dirty clothes,' he said. 'Need to stick them in the washer.'

He looked up and gazed, bleary-eyed, at Matt. 'Hello. Do I know you?'

Matt said with a wry smile, 'No, I don't think so. I'm Matt. I work with Sasha.'

'Oh. I see.' Sam stuck out a hand that didn't quite synchronise with Matt's. 'I'm Sasha's brother. I'll see you. Got to go and lie down.'

Sam lurched away, and Sasha stared after him. What on earth was wrong with him?

Matt must have read her glance because he said quietly, 'I can see that you're worried about him. He's a student, isn't he? He doesn't look well. Has he complained of feeling ill?'

'No. He sounded fine when I spoke to him on the phone the other day.'

'He doesn't look it now.' Matt studied her thoughtfully. 'Do you think he could be taking drugs?'

Her glance swivelled to him. 'No,' she said vehemently. 'He wouldn't do that.'

'Are you sure of that? He looks in a pretty bad way. I've seen students in that condition before.'

'There could be other reasons for him to be in the state he's in. He's probably just overtired after too many late nights, studying for his pharmacy exams. He works in the student bar, and I expect he's been staying up after that to study. Do you think I don't know my own brother? I've looked after him for years. I know him better than anyone.'

Her eyes flashed a warning and her tone was sharp,

reflecting the stress she was under. 'I don't know what's wrong with him, but I know it can't be anything like drugs. He wouldn't take them.'

He wouldn't, would he? She had been so certain, but now Matt was putting doubts in her mind.

All at once everything crowded in on her. For years she had taken on the burden of caring for her mother and making sure that her brother was protected. Even now he was older, she was looking out for him, knowing that his start in life had been difficult. It was a lonely task. She loved them both, but there were times when she felt as though she carried the world on her shoulders. Now her mother was seriously ill all over again and she was desperately worried for her.

Why was it that all her efforts came to nothing? Her mouth trembled and she tried to clamp it still.

Matt moved towards her. 'This is all too much for you, isn't it? If there's anything I can do, you know that I'm here. You don't have to struggle on alone. Let me help.'

Tears stung her eyes and she blinked them away, not wanting him to see them. He drew her close, wrapping his arms around her. 'I'm sorry,' he said. 'I didn't mean to upset you. Of course you know your own brother.'

His closeness, the intimacy of having his strong arms hold her, shattered her fragile defences. She drank in the warmth and comfort of his embrace like a flower that had gone without water for too long. His shoulder was there for her and the temptation was too great to resist. As his hand curved around the back of her head and tangled with the silk of her hair, she leaned her cheek against his chest for a moment, absorbing the shelter he offered.

His breathing was strong and steady, and his arms held her firmly. She wanted to stay like this for a long while, to be soothed and cherished, but she knew that she couldn't. Her mother needed her.

Besides, it wouldn't do, would it, to turn to Matt for reassurance? He was only going to be there for a moment, and anyway he was her boss, not her comfort blanket. He already believed she wasn't on top of things at work after the way things had gone wrong this morning with little Kimberley, and it would be a disaster if she fell apart now. She couldn't give him any more reason for having misgivings about her.

There was no one she could rely on to be there for her through all her troubles. Even her own father had left her behind and hadn't she learned a long time ago that she was better off sorting things out for herself?

She laid a hand flatly, shakily, against Matt's ribcage and eased herself away from him. 'I'm sorry,' she said. 'I'm not usually as weak as this. I think I'm just tired and out of sorts. I'll be fine.'

'I mean it,' he said. 'If there's anything I can do…'

'No. I'll deal with it. Anyway, I have to go back upstairs to my mother.' She had to be strong and independent. It was safer that way, and things were less likely to fall apart.

She ran a hand through her hair. 'The doctor should be here soon to see her. I'll go and have a word with Josh. I'm sorry to cut his visit short. If he's upset about going so soon, perhaps he can come another day when things are less fraught?'

Matt didn't answer, but he seemed to have straightened up, and his body had stiffened a little. He looked at her, his eyes dark and unreadable, and she wondered what was going through his mind. Was he put out because she had pushed him away? She winced. Like it or not, it was the way it had to be.

CHAPTER FIVE

'I'LL stay until the doctor has looked at your mother,' Matt said. 'You might need some help and, whether you like it or not, I can't just turn my back on the situation. If your mother is ill enough to need oxygen, then there may be other developments.'

Sasha pulled air into her lungs. 'I didn't mean to put you to any trouble. You were doubtful about coming here with Josh in the first place.'

'Well, I'm here now, so I'll hang around until I know everything's under control.'

'All right.' She glanced at him. She was relieved that she wasn't on her own in this. 'Will you make sure that Josh is occupied while I go and check on her? There are paper and pencils in the kitchen drawer. He can have those if he wants to make some pictures.'

He nodded, and his mobile phone rang at that moment. He started to answer it, and she turned away and headed towards the stairs. She heard him say, 'No, I'm sorry. I forgot that you had to go out. I'm at Sasha's house, across the park. Something's cropped up. Do you want to bring them over here to me?'

She had no idea what he was talking about, and her immediate concern was for her mother. Why wouldn't the doctor hurry up and get here? If she didn't arrive soon, she would take it into her own hands to treat her mother.

Sam was asleep on the bed in his own room, and Sasha shut the door on him and went to her mother's side. 'Thanks, Theresa,' she said. 'I'll take over with the oxygen. Do you want to get off home? I'm sorry to have kept you here so long.'

Theresa shook her head. 'I want to stay and see that she's all right...if you don't mind?'

Sasha gave a brief, taut smile. 'Thanks. Yes, that's OK.'

'Is there anything you need?'

'I think my mother would be able to breathe better if I had some nebulised salbutamol. You could ask Matt...Dr Benton...if he has any in his car. He's downstairs.'

'I'll do that.' Theresa hurried away.

'Hold on there, Mum,' Sasha said quietly, taking over the ventilation. 'The doctor's on her way, and we'll soon have you feeling more comfortable. My boss is downstairs. I think he might be able to help, if that's all right with you?'

Her mother didn't answer, but she gave an almost imperceptible nod, and soon after that there was a knock at the door and Matt came in, carrying a portable nebuliser.

'Hello, Mrs Rushford,' he said, giving her mother a smile. 'I'm Matt, a colleague of Sasha's. I've brought something with me that should help your chest to feel a little easier.'

He set up the nebuliser and after a while Sasha saw that her mother was looking a little less stressed. Theresa came back into the room and said, 'I've given Josh some things to play with, but he's asking for you, Sasha. I'll sit with Ellen if you like.'

Sasha frowned, but her mother nodded and took the mask off her face, saying in a halting way, 'You go. You can answer the door…to the doctor…when she comes.'

Sasha was doubtful about leaving her, but Matt stood up to go with her, and she finally left the room.

'I think you should get your mother to hospital now,' Matt said in a low voice, 'and not wait for the doctor. She's in a bad way.'

'I'm not sure,' Sasha muttered. 'She's stable right now, and the doctor should be here at any moment.' Even as she spoke, the doorbell rang, and Sasha went to open it.

Matt's father was there. 'I'm sorry to turn up at a time like this,' he said. 'Matt told me over the phone that your mother was ill. I had to bring some clothes over to Matt for little Josh, though. He'll need them for school tomorrow, and I have to go out shortly.' He placed a holdall on the hall floor.

He hesitated, then added, 'I know your mother. I've seen her about the village. She's a lovely lady and I'm really sorry to hear that she's ill again. Is there anything I can do to help?'

Sasha shook her head. 'Nothing, just now, thanks all the same. I think we have everything pretty much under control.'

'Her mother's almost in a state of collapse,' Matt said. 'I've told Sasha that we shouldn't wait any longer, but we should get her to hospital.'

Matt's father glanced at her. 'Don't you agree?'

Sasha felt as though she was being cornered on two fronts. Matt could have a point, though. He was a consultant after all, and she didn't want to take any risks with her mother's health.

'I'm expecting her GP to arrive at any moment, and I'm reluctant to take over from her. She's the one who is treating my mother.' Sasha hesitated. It was a question of correct procedure, but the GP had already delayed over the antibiotics, and perhaps that delay had caused her mother's condition to worsen. She didn't want to take any more risks. 'Perhaps Matt's right, though. I'll call for an ambulance.'

A few minutes later the doctor arrived, and Sasha hurried to show her to her mother's room.

Dr Shaw examined her mother carefully, then put her stethoscope in her pocket and turned to Sasha. 'I think you were right in your diagnosis. It is pneumonia, and it's too serious for her to be nursed at home. She'll have to go to hospital. We'll keep your mother on oxygen, and get her there by ambulance.'

Turning back to Sasha's mother, she said, 'Just try to relax, and let us do everything. You'll be well looked after in hospital. They'll need to do a chest X-ray and blood tests.'

'I've already called the ambulance,' Sasha said. 'I didn't want to wait.'

'That's good. The sooner we get her transferred,

the better. I'll stay here and see that she's all right, if you want to go and get some things together for her.'

Sasha filled a small overnight bag and went to tell Matt what was happening. 'Thanks for helping me out,' she said. 'The salbutamol seems to have eased her breathing.'

'I was glad to be able to do something.'

The ambulance arrived within a couple of minutes, and as the paramedics hurried upstairs, Sasha said, 'I'm going to go with her in the ambulance and see her settled into hospital.'

'You'll need a lift back,' Matt murmured. 'I'll follow in my car, and make sure that you get back safely.'

'There's no need for you to do that.' She couldn't ask him to help her out any more when he already had Josh to look after. Besides, Sasha was beginning to feel frazzled. So much had happened in the short time since she had come home from work—her mother was dangerously ill, her brother was behaving oddly, and now her house was filled with people, all wanting to do their bit. Their kindness was a blessing, but she was too overwrought to appreciate it right now. 'I can manage,' she said.

The last thing she needed was to let Matt take the burden from her. She had already come dangerously close to turning to him for comfort, and it would never do to come to need him. That way could only lead to hurt.

'I don't think you should try to manage on your own.' Matt looked at her directly. 'You're shaky and obviously in no state to drive yourself, and I see no reason why you should get a taxi home when I can drive you. Besides, you've filled an overnight bag. I can take that in my car.'

She stared at him. Why was the man so determined? It didn't help when inside she was yearning to give in. 'It's not necessary,' she murmured. 'Besides, you have Josh to think of.' Matt's father was chatting with Josh right now, but she was conscious that he was close at hand.

'He'll enjoy it. He'll think he's having an adventure.' Gently, he added, 'You have to learn to accept help when it's offered.'

'I don't see why,' she retorted. 'I didn't see you rushing to accept when I offered to help out with Josh.'

'That's different. I'm a man, and I don't have the worries that you have. Nothing is going very well for you at the moment, is it? You have a lot to contend with, and you shouldn't have to do it on your own. It will affect everything—your work, your health.'

So she was just a helpless woman who couldn't sort her life out, was she? For as far back as she could remember she had struggled to stay on top of things, to cope with whatever life threw her way. It was the only way she knew to survive.

She was in no mood to argue with him, though, especially in front of his father and Theresa. Instead, she let her gaze speak volumes.

'I don't want you to go with me to the hospital,' she said firmly. 'I don't know how long I'm going to stay there, and it's too late to keep Josh up. I'd really prefer to see this through by myself. I'm sorry that things haven't turned out as I expected for Josh, but at least he seems to have enjoyed himself up to now, and he's oblivious to what is going on.'

Matt gave her a hard stare. William came over and said, 'I'll wish your mother well, and then I have to be on my way. I've an appointment to keep. A nuisance, but it can't be avoided.'

Sasha smiled wanly, and hurried upstairs to supervise her mother's transfer. True to his word, as they made to leave the house, William clasped her mother's hand in his.

'Ellen, I'm so sorry that you're ill. I'll be thinking of you,' he said. 'You take care. I'll come and visit you in hospital as soon as you're up to it.'

'Thank you, William.' Her mother leaned her head back against her pillows as though the effort had been too much for her. William watched her being wheeled into the ambulance and waved, before going on his way. Theresa left, too.

Sasha gave Josh a quick cuddle and said goodbye to Matt. He stood by as she hurried to sit beside her mother. His expression was unreadable. Josh waved, smiling, not knowing what was going on.

Her brother was still asleep, and she had left him a note to say what was happening. There was no point in getting him involved.

She saw her mother settled onto a ward. 'We'll do blood tests and get a chest X-ray,' the doctor on duty told her. 'In the meantime, we'll give her IV fluids along with analgesia and a different antibiotic.'

'Thank you. I'll sit with her for a while, if that's all right.'

She stayed with her mother until darkness fell and then returned home. Sam was still asleep, and Sasha wondered what on earth had made him so exhausted.

At the hospital the next afternoon, Matt frowned as he saw her coming in to work. 'I didn't expect to see you here today. Shouldn't you be with your mother?' he asked.

'I was, most of yesterday evening and all of this morning, but she's asleep now, and I wanted to keep busy. I'm better off at work.'

'I'm not so sure about that.' Matt stared at her, his eyes narrowing. 'There are dark circles under your eyes.'

'I'll cover them with make-up,' she retorted.

'What about your brother? Doesn't he need you?'

'He's fine.' Sam had still not surfaced by the time she'd left for the hospital this morning, and Theresa had said she would talk to him later. Sasha was glad of that. Perhaps she could find out what was wrong with him.

Matt was still studying her through narrowed eyes. 'If you find things too much for you, you should let me know. It can't be easy doing your job when you have worries at the back of your mind.'

'You don't need to be concerned about that. I won't let anything get in the way of my work.' His comment bothered her, though she was trying not to show it.

Did he think she would make a mistake? How could she prove to him that she was perfectly capable of doing her job?

A man was brought in just a moment later, and Sasha hurried to attend to him. She tried to put her conversation with Matt to the back of her mind.

James Radcliffe was a farmer, in his late forties, his face weathered by years of working out in the open. He had suffered a bad crush injury to his left hand.

'How did this happen, James?' Sasha asked.

The man gritted his teeth. He was white with shock, but he was still conscious and Sasha hoped he would be able to fill in some of the details.

'I was inspecting the machinery on the back of my tractor. It had stuck, and I wanted to free it up.' He sucked in a deep breath as she examined the injury.

'I'll give you another painkilling injection and a tetanus jab,' she said. 'The analgesia should make you feel a little easier.' She worked carefully and quickly. 'Go on with what you were saying,' she murmured. 'I'm still not sure what happened to you.'

'I saw some young lads messing about. I tried to see what they were doing, but they ran away. When I turned back to the machinery it slipped and did this. Am I going to lose the hand?'

'I can't really say what will happen right now,' Sasha said cautiously. 'I've asked for a surgeon to come down and look at your hand. I'm pretty sure that you'll need to go up to Theatre, and it may be that Mr Danby can repair damaged nerves, tendons and so on. We'll have to wait and see how things progress. Mr Danby is a good man, one of the best, and he'll look after you, I'm sure.' She was worried that James might lose the hand altogether, but she wasn't going to tell him that.

She could see that the farmer was troubled. 'Are you left-handed or right-handed?' she asked.

'I'm right-handed—I suppose that's something. If the surgeon can save the hand, at least I might be able to do my job even if the left hand doesn't work so well.' He dragged in another shaky breath. 'How long will it take before I can be back at work?'

'I don't think you should worry about that right now. Is there anyone who can help out at the farm?'

'My son, perhaps. I'll have to ask him to help out for a while and maybe bring someone in.'

He was still very anxious, and Sasha said, 'If the surgeon can repair the injuries, it will take some time for the tissues to heal, and then you would need to have physiotherapy to restore the function. At this stage it's really hard to say what the outcome will be. I'm sorry.'

She signalled to a nurse. 'I'm going to ask the nurse to stay with you and answer any other questions you might have. In the meantime, I'll give you antibiotics to help prevent any infection.'

She glanced at him before she left the bedside. 'Is there anything else I can do for you? Is there anyone we need to contact?'

He shook his head. 'My wife is coming in.

Someone phoned her. She was out when this happened.'

Sasha glanced at him. 'I suppose the boys were playing after school. Do they often come onto the farm?'

'Sometimes. They get in through the orchard.'

'Good luck with the surgery,' Sasha said. 'I'll come back and see you later.' She felt sorry for the man. It was a bad injury, and even if Mr Danby could repair things, it was fairly clear that the farmer would suffer some residual weakness in the hand.

Matt joined her as she made her way towards the cafeteria later that day. 'I saw your patient going up to surgery a short time ago,' he said. 'Have you any idea what the outcome will be?'

Sasha reached for a tray and inspected the shelves, looking for a snack to go along with her coffee. 'I think Mr Danby was going to see if it was possible to save the man's hand. He said amputation would be the last resort. He's not sure how much function he can restore, and it would all depend on how the healing goes.' She glanced at Matt. 'It's terrible when your livelihood depends on your hands, isn't it?'

'I suppose that applies to most of us in some way,' he said. He helped himself to a bun and an apple. 'From what I hear, the boys who caused the distraction are very upset. The youngest one, a nine-year-old, thinks he might have been responsible for what happened to him.'

Sasha's brows lifted. 'Why would he think that? How do you know?'

'His mother came in to see how Mr Radcliffe was getting on. She said the boy was distraught.'

'But he didn't cause the accident, surely?'

'The boy thinks that because he distracted him, the farmer didn't take care to look what he was doing.'

'Has his mother explained things to him?'

'I'm not sure. I think he ran off, in case he was going to get into trouble.'

Sasha picked out a cake and a dish of fruit salad. 'It's very sad, isn't it? Just one action or a moment's carelessness can have devastating results.' She paid for her food, and Matt did likewise and joined her at a table by the window. 'It's going to be very hard for both Mr Radcliffe and the boys to come to terms with what happened. The boys will blame themselves even if they weren't actually responsible.'

He nodded and was quiet for a moment, mulling things over. His face was serious, and Sasha said, 'Is something bothering you?'

He sent her a quick glance. 'Not about your patient, but his situation has made me wonder about the boys' reactions to what happened. I think in a way Josh feels the same way the nine-year-old does. He thinks that he's responsible, that he's the reason why his mother left home. He keeps asking me if he's been a bad boy. He keeps saying he will be good, if only his mother will come back.'

Matt's expression was sombre, and Sasha reached out and covered his hand with her own. 'I'm so sorry. Is there anything you can do to get her back?'

'I'm still trying to think of anywhere she might

have gone. I've tried the local hotels and guesthouses, and I've put notices up. The police are looking for her, and the Salvation Army. So far no one's come up with anything.'

'You must be feeling awful. Is there any chance of the father, Josh's father, helping out?'

He shook his head. 'I think he's the cause of the whole thing, to be honest. He never wanted children, and for some reason he thought Helen had tricked him by becoming pregnant. I'm sure she didn't but, all the same, he treated her badly. He made her feel as though she was worthless. She started to sink into depression, and she began to doubt herself. I think that's why she left. She had already been suffering from postnatal depression, and things went from bad to worse. She didn't feel that she could be a good mother to Josh. She thought that he would be better off without her.'

Sasha was troubled. 'Didn't you try to talk to her about the way she was thinking?'

'Of course I did. It didn't make any difference, but I had no idea that she would take into her head to leave.'

'Where is her husband now?'

'Ex-husband. He was more intent on following his career than he was on keeping the marriage going. He's working abroad now.'

Sasha was quiet for a moment. She stirred her coffee, and took a bite of her cake. Then she said, 'I think I can understand something of what Josh is going through. I was in a similar situation when I was a child and my mother became ill. She had to go into hospital for a long time, and I was very confused about things, worried about what the outcome was going to be.'

She winced. 'My father couldn't cope. I had the feeling that the marriage started to fall apart as she became ill, and I don't think he could take in what was happening. He seemed to retreat into his own world. He concentrated on his work more than anything. I was eleven or twelve at the time, and my brother, Sam, was five or six, so it must have been worse for him. We muddled through somehow.'

'How long did that go on for?'

'It's hard to say. A long time. In the end he left us, and I felt that it was the ultimate betrayal. He left my mother while she was still in hospital, and we went to stay with an aunt for a time, but she had her own family, and she was out at work in the daytime. Mostly, I looked out for my brother.'

'That must have been difficult.'

'I didn't think about it. When my mother came out of hospital, she wasn't strong, and I did what I could to make things easy for her. It came to be a way of life. I still remember how it felt, though, to be abandoned. My mother had no choice because she was ill, but my father did. I've never spoken to him since then.'

Matt looked at her steadily, his grey eyes thoughtful. 'Is that why you want to help out with Josh? Because you identify with him?'

She nodded. 'I think so...probably. He's a wonderful little boy, and I hate to see him sad.' She sipped her coffee and added, 'Will you let me help with him?'

'You have enough on your plate at the moment, with your mother and your brother.'

'Even so…'

He shook his head. 'Josh is my problem, not yours. You have enough worries of your own to contend with.'

'Aren't you being a trifle stubborn over this? I wouldn't be offering if I didn't think I could manage.'

'I know you mean well, Sasha. I don't think I have time to discuss this right now, though.' He glanced at his watch. 'I should get back to the department. I'm due at a meeting in half an hour, and I've some things to clear up before then.'

'Is this a management meeting?'

'That's right. It's to do with the problems of recruitment and so on.'

'If you're not sure how to go about it,' she said cheekily, 'you could always suggest that they try to employ more women doctors, on a part-time basis. I'm sure there must be an untapped source out there.'

His mouth curved. 'I'll be sure and tell them that.'

He was at the meeting when it was time for Sasha's shift to end. She called in on her mother, and sat with her for a while, before making her way home. Her condition was not improving, and she didn't speak very much. Sasha saw that she was being given fluids and that she was still on oxygen.

'I can see that you're very tired, Mum,' Sasha said.

'I'll leave you to get some rest. I've left some music tapes with you, in case you feel like listening to them. There's a story tape, too. One of your favourite authors. I'm sure the nurses will set them up for you.'

She moved away from the bedside and went to the nurses' station to ask for an update on her mother's treatment.

'We're still trying to find the organism responsible,' the nurse in charge told her. 'Until we've found it, we're giving her broad-spectrum antibiotics.'

'They don't seem to be working very well,' Sasha said.

'I know,' the nurse answered, 'but these are early days yet.'

There was nothing more Sasha could do, and she decided to go home and try and get through some of her chores. Sam was up and about, but his mood was scratchy.

'You should have woken me before you went out today,' he said. 'I didn't know that Mum was so ill that she needed to go to hospital.'

'I tried to wake you,' Sasha said. 'You weren't having any of it.'

'I had a lot of catching up to do,' he said, more soberly this time. 'I've had a lot of late nights lately, and I was exhausted. That's why I came home. I thought at least I might get some work done here, without interruption.'

'Are things not going well at university? I thought you liked staying on campus?'

'Most of the time I do.' He grimaced, and changed

the subject. 'I called in to see Mum this afternoon, but she was in a bad way.'

'Try not to worry,' Sasha said. 'The doctors are doing everything they can for her.' She was worried about the situation, but she didn't see why Sam had to take on any more just now. He was obviously troubled by something that was going on at university.

The phone rang, and it was a girl wanting to speak to Sam. She sounded young and excitable and desperate to talk to him. Sasha handed over the phone, and just at that moment the doorbell sounded.

She opened the door and saw that Matt was standing there, holding Josh's hand.

Sasha's face lit up in a smile. 'Matt…Josh, how lovely to see you.' She crouched down to be on a level with Josh, and he grinned widely in return.

'I wanted to come see you,' Josh said.

'I'm so glad that you did.' She straightened up and opened the door wider, ushering him into the hall.

'Does that greeting include me?' Matt said, his tone wry.

'Of course. I'm just a little surprised to see you, that's all.' She could hardly take it in that he was here. He was dressed in casual clothes, chinos and a fresh shirt that was open at the collar so that she caught a glimpse of his lightly bronzed throat. He looked good.

'Josh wanted to bring something for you,' Matt said.

Sasha looked at Josh and saw that he was hiding

something behind his back. 'I bringed you some flowers,' the little boy said, producing them with a flourish.

'Oh, aren't they beautiful?' Sasha said, accepting the colourful posy with a smile. 'Thank you, Josh. I'll go and put them in some water. Shall we go through to the kitchen?'

'Can I play on the swing?' Josh asked.

'Of course you can. You know the way, don't you?'

Josh was already racing for the kitchen door, and Matt followed, keeping track of him. As Sasha passed by Sam, she heard him say, 'No, Lucy. I'm not going to do this any more. I don't care what you're going through. I've had enough. You can forget it.' He slammed the receiver down.

'Is something wrong?' Sasha asked, stopping to look at him in concern. She placed the posy of flowers on the hall table. She was shocked by what he had said. 'Is there anything you want to talk to me about?'

'Nothing's wrong.'

'The girl was very anxious to talk to you when I spoke to her. Is she a girlfriend?'

'She works with me in the students' union bar. She's ditzy and she likes to party. You don't need to know about her.'

'Is she the one who's been making you lose sleep? Is that why you're worried about your exams? Perhaps you've been partying with her?'

'I told you—there's nothing you need to know about. I don't see why you should try to prise things out of me. I don't want to talk about it.' Sam grabbed his jacket from the cloakroom and the front door banged behind him as he left the house.

Sasha stared after him, upset by his outburst. What was that all about?

Matt said quietly behind her, 'He'll calm down, given time.'

'Will he? I'm not so sure about that.' Her voice broke. 'I don't know what's happening to him. He isn't the brother I know. He used to confide in me.'

Matt moved closer to her. 'Things look bleak right now because you're tired and distressed. You're trying to cope with things raining down on you, and it's hard when there seem to be no answers. It won't always be this way. You need to take a deep breath and slow down. You can handle this.'

She shook her head. 'I don't think I can. I've never seen him this way before. The way he spoke to that girl was so harsh and uncaring.' Her eyes filled with tears and she blinked them away. Why was everything going wrong?

Matt's arms closed around her, folding her to him. 'Are you afraid that he's going to turn out like your father?'

How could he reach into her mind like that and draw out her innermost thoughts? Her mouth trembled. 'He can't. I know him better than that. Why won't he talk to me?'

Matt held her tight, as though he would keep her safe, secure. 'He's young, and he's confused. He's trying to study for his exams, and it looks as though he has girl trouble as well. It sounds as if he's going through a difficult time, but you shouldn't give up on him. I'm sure things will look better in a day or so.'

Sasha sniffed. 'I hope so.'

He stroked her hair, his fingers threading through the bright mass of her curls. 'Trust me, they will. You're weary. You've had a long day at work and you need to wind down. Don't let this get to you.'

He curved his hand beneath her chin and tilted her face so that she was looking directly at him. 'Give me a smile. Just a little one.'

His eyes were warm and tender, and she felt as though he was drawing her in out of the cold. She tried to do as he asked, her mouth making the faintest of movements, and his head lowered, his lips brushing hers.

It was a gentle kiss, a soft, explorative caress, as though he was testing the fullness of her mouth against his, but it startled her, throwing her completely off guard. She responded without thinking, her lips tingling, on fire, craving his touch, and she leaned into him, absorbing the delicious sensation of his mouth on hers.

His hands stroked along her spine, leaving a trail of flame in their wake. 'I'm here for you,' he murmured. 'You're not on your own in this.'

He kissed her again, more thoroughly this time, his lips pressuring hers, his hands moving over her, gliding over her soft curves in a journey of discovery. Her whole body quivered with a sudden intensity of feeling as he drew her against him.

'Uncle Matt…Uncle Matt. I found a pebble. Come and see…'

Sasha stiffened as the piping voice came closer. She had forgotten everything in those last few moments. What was she thinking of, giving herself up to Matt's kisses and losing track of time and place?

She pulled away from him, hardly daring to look up at him. 'I should have gone after Josh,' she muttered. 'It isn't fair to leave him to his own devices.'

Matt reluctantly let her go and straightened his shoulders. 'You're right. That was thoughtless of me.' His glance moved over her. 'He was desperate to come here and see you. I didn't mean for this to happen. Perhaps it would have been better if I'd stayed away.'

'I'm glad you brought him. I feel so sorry that his mother isn't around.'

His mouth made a straight line. 'Me, too.' He turned around and went to meet Josh. 'Come on, little man. Let's have a look at this pebble.'

'It's beautiful,' she heard Josh say. 'It's got lots of colours. Can I give it to Mummy?'

Sasha didn't hear Matt's answer. She closed her eyes briefly to shut out the intrusion, remembering the way Matt had held her, as though he would be her support, her safeguard against life's worries. It wasn't going to happen that way, though, was it? Why would he want to look out for her? He wasn't going to be staying around for long, given his track record. His driving force was his career, the constant search for the next step up the ladder.

It would be a mistake to lean on him, wouldn't it? How many other women had done the same and been left behind? She didn't want to count herself as one of that number.

CHAPTER SIX

'WE SHOULD go,' Matt said. 'Time's getting on and I have some things to do this evening.'

Josh's face crumpled. 'Sasha gave me some san'wiches,' he said.

'I know, but when you've finished eating, we must be on our way. I promised Grandad I'd take you over to his house for a while.'

Josh brightened. 'Will my mummy be there?'

Matt looked sad. 'No, Josh. Not today. We're still trying to find your mummy.' He knelt down beside the boy, to be on a level with him. 'We're looking everywhere we can think of.' After a moment, he said, 'You like going to visit Grandad, don't you? He said he would let you do some woodwork with him if you like.'

'Yes!' Josh's mood changed like quicksilver. 'We made a cart with wheels,' he confided to Sasha.

'I expect you'll make something just as good today.' Matt stood up and glanced at Sasha. 'Thanks for giving us tea,' he said, 'but we really need to be going now.'

'That's all right. Any time.' She was still subdued after what had happened earlier. The kiss had been unexpected and far more overwhelming than she might ever have imagined. It had been a mistake, of course, a moment of madness, and she doubted Matt would follow it up.

A little while later, as she saw them out of the front door, Matt said, 'I'll see you at work tomorrow.' He paused. 'I spoke to Mr Danby about the farmer whose hand he operated on. He sounded reasonably hopeful that the man would recover some use of the hand.'

'That's good.' She added quietly, 'Was there any news of the boy from the farm? Ryan, I think his name is. I heard on the local news that he had gone missing.'

Matt shook his head. 'As far as I know, he's still not turned up. His mother said Ryan was afraid that he would be blamed for the accident, and when he was told that the farmer was being operated on, he was worried that the man would lose his hand. He didn't stay around to find out what had come of the surgery.'

'Have they any idea where he might be?' She was worried about the boy.

'I don't think so. His mother thought he'd gone out to be with his friends, but they haven't seen him, and when he didn't come home when he was supposed to, she reported him missing.'

She grimaced. 'It's getting late now, and it will soon be dark. He must be feeling distraught to stay away for so long. It sounds as though the police are taking things seriously.'

'I think they have to. There are rivers and lakes around here, and he could be in danger. I suppose they'll be searching the fields all around. There must be all sorts of places where he could hide.'

'That's true. I hope they find him before night falls. It can get very cold out in the open, and he's just a young lad. He wasn't wearing a coat, just jeans and T-shirt from what I heard.'

Josh tugged at Matt's hand, bored with waiting around. 'I want to see Grandad,' he said. 'Come on, Uncle Matt.'

Matt gave Sasha a dry smile. 'Well, there's a turn-around. Just a few minutes ago he was upset because he wasn't going to be staying here.'

'That's children for you. They're fickle.' Sasha watched the two of them leave in Matt's sleek car, and then she went back into the house. She felt out of sorts, at odds with herself, and she knew that Matt was the reason for her discomfort. He had shown her what it was like to be cherished, if only for a brief moment, and she longed for more of the same. The feeling unsettled her. What was the point in hoping that Matt would come to care for her? His reaction had just been a spur-of-the-moment thing, an impulse, nothing more. Why was she even thinking this way?

She made up her mind to put him from her thoughts, but that was no easy thing to do. Somehow she had to keep busy, and perhaps the best way to do that would be to join the search for the missing boy. How far could he have gone in just a few hours?

Pulling on a jacket and stuffing a few essential items into a holdall, she left the house and went to the place where the search was being organised. They had taken over a church hall as their headquarters. A rescue team was out in force, checking out all the places where a child might hide. Sasha approached the co-ordinator and asked what she could do to help.

'We're checking the fields and the hedgerows for the lad,' the police officer said. 'Any barns in the area have already been searched, but we'll go back to them again later. You could try the northeast corner by the old farm cottage. There are one or two people out there already—I'm sending all the latecomers over there. We're really glad of your help—every pair of eyes helps. Get in touch with us by phone if you find anything.'

'I will.' Sasha set off along the country lane, heading towards the meadow. In the distance, she could see the white-painted farm cottage, and she decided that she would make that her starting point.

By now it was late evening, and a chill breeze was blowing, and she was glad that she had thought to put on jeans and a warm sweater. It was beginning to get dark. The leaves on the trees all around rustled and whispered, and she wondered how little Ryan was faring. He must be frightened.

As she approached the cottage, she stood for a moment and looked around at the rolling hills and valleys. If she were a small boy, where would she go and hide? Trees and hedgerows would make good cover, and perhaps that was where she would go first.

She walked quickly over the meadow and down the hillside, heading for a clump of overgrown trees, but she came to a stop when she saw that someone was already there. The man must have heard her approach, because he turned and glanced towards her.

'Sasha? What are you doing here?' Matt sounded surprised.

Sasha's eyes widened. Her spirits lifted as soon as she saw that it was really him. 'I could ask you the same thing. I thought you were at your father's house with Josh.'

'I was, for a while, but I left him there. He's going to stay overnight. I felt I had to come and look for the little boy. It worries me to think of him being out here at night.'

'Me, too.' Sasha walked towards Matt, her pulse quickening for no reason that she could think of. 'No one's had any luck so far. I've checked all the hedgerows on the way down here, and I've been calling Ryan's name, but there's been no sight or sound of him up to now.'

'I was just going to check the bushes, down by the brook. Shall we look for him together? You might see or hear something that I miss. That way, we can help each other.'

'That's a good idea.' She was glad that she wasn't on her own, and she was more than thankful that Matt was to be her companion. She felt that she could rely on him, that he was strong and capable, and that with him by her side she could achieve anything.

They searched for over an hour, scrabbling through undergrowth, pushing aside overhanging branches of trees, stopping every now and again to call Ryan's name through the darkness.

Matt said, 'I think we should take a break for a while. Let's go and sit by the edge of the lake. I brought a flask of coffee with me. It will warm us a little.'

Sasha agreed. By the lake, there were the stumps of trees that had been cut down, and they sat on them, sipping at the coffee, looking around. Matt placed his backpack down on the ground, and then took his mobile phone from his pocket and called in to find out if there had been any news.

He pushed the phone back into his pocket. 'No one has found him yet,' he said. His mouth was straight, and there was a far-away look in his eyes. Sasha could guess what he was thinking. He must have gone through this with his sister.

'We can't give up,' she said. 'We must find him.'

'His mother must be going through hell.' He was silent, thinking, his gaze bleak.

Sasha said softly, 'You must be worrying about your sister, too. Have you had any luck tracing her?'

'Not so far. I've tried to think of all the places that Helen might have gone—holiday homes, places we lived in before we moved down here. I haven't been able to come up with anything.' He grimaced. 'Every day Josh asks me when she's coming home, and I can't give him an answer.'

Sasha went over to him. She knelt beside him and put her arms around him, giving him a hug. 'I'm so sorry. I wish there was something I could do.'

He squeezed her hand. 'At least we can go on looking for young Ryan. There's still a chance that we might find him.'

He got to his feet, and Sasha walked with him alongside the lake. He switched on his torch and shone the beam of light all around. 'Ryan...where are you, boy? We want to help you. You're not in any trouble. Shout out if you can hear us.' They stopped and listened, but there was no sound to break the silence. They moved on.

After a while, Sasha said, 'I think I can just make out a hollowed-out tree over there in that little clearing. I want to go and take a look.'

Matt went with her, shining the beam of the torch all around. 'What's that?' he said. 'Do you see? Over by the tree trunk...'

Together, they went to investigate. Sasha said anxiously, 'Matt, we've found him. This must be Ryan.' The child was huddled against the foot of the tree. She knelt down and touched him.

'Ryan,' she said. 'Ryan, can you hear me?' The boy didn't answer.

Looking up at Matt, she said, 'His clothes are wet through. He must have fallen in the water at some point. He feels very cold.'

Matt came and knelt beside her. He took a stethoscope from his backpack and began to listen to the boy's chest, while she phoned the rescue team to say that they had found the child. 'His heartbeat's way too slow,' he said, 'and his breathing is irregular.'

'We should get him warmed up as quickly as possible.' Sasha began to take off her jacket, but Matt stopped her.

'He can have my jacket,' he said. 'I'll take these wet clothes off him and then we should get some warm fluids inside him.'

'I brought some hot chocolate with me,' Sasha said. 'I thought it might come in useful if we found him. I'll cool it down a little before I give it to him.'

'That was good thinking,' Matt murmured as she took out a flask from her bag. He worked quickly, removing the child's top clothes and replacing them with his sweater and jacket. 'We'll soon have you warmed up,' he told the boy.

He held him gently while Sasha put a cup of warm liquid to the child's lips. 'Try to drink this, Ryan,' she said softly.

Slowly she got the liquid into him, and after a while the boy's eyes flickered. He looked at her, trying to make sense of what was going on. In the end, he must have realised where he was.

'I can't go home,' he managed through stiff lips.

'Your parents are very worried about you,' Sasha said. 'You mustn't be afraid to go home. You haven't done anything wrong.'

'I made the farmer hurt himself,' Ryan said, tears filling his eyes. 'I didn't mean it. We were just play-ing.'

'He doesn't blame you,' Matt said. 'He told me that something had come loose at the back of the tractor, and that's why the equipment fell onto his hand. It would have happened anyway, even if you boys hadn't been there.'

Ryan's eyes grew large. 'I didn't hurt him?' he asked. He looked to Sasha for confirmation.

'It wasn't your fault,' she said.

In the distance, they heard the sound of rescuers approaching. Everything moved quickly after that. Paramedics came and transferred the boy to a stretcher and took him away. He was reunited with his mother and then he was taken to hospital, where his condition could be monitored.

Sasha walked back through the fields with Matt, and then he went with her to her car. 'I don't see your car anywhere around,' she said, puzzled.

'It's still at my father's house. A neighbour came by and when I said I wanted to come and help with the search he offered me a lift here.' He made a wry face. 'He seems to have gone home without me.'

'That's no problem—I'll give you a lift,' she offered.

The journey only took a few minutes. His father's house was in the next village to theirs, a beautiful stone-built house, with a welcoming lantern in the porch and a cottage garden that was coming into bloom.

William opened the door to them. 'You found the boy, then? I'm so pleased about that. I've been sitting here, worrying.'

They went through to the living room, and Matt said, 'Did I just hear Josh calling out? Isn't he asleep yet?'

His father shook his head. 'I put him to bed some time ago, but he's been very restless. I've sat with him, read stories to him, but he doesn't seem to be able to settle. He was finally dozing, but he must have heard the front door.'

'I'm sorry if we woke him,' Sasha said. 'We tried to be quiet.'

'It's not your fault,' William said with a smile. 'Go up and see him, if you like. He talks about you all the while. He'll be glad to see you, and you might be able to get him to settle better than I can. I'll fix us all a pot of tea and some sandwiches while you're up there. You must both be starving.'

Sasha looked at Matt. 'Is it all right with you if I go up and see him?' she asked.

Matt nodded. 'I'll come up with you. He was asking me about young Ryan. I expect he'll want to know what's gone on.'

Josh sat up in bed and rubbed his eyes as Sasha went quietly into his room. 'It's you,' he said, his mouth breaking into a smile. 'I wanted to see you.'

'I thought you would be fast asleep by now,' Sasha murmured, going over to him and sitting down on the edge of the bed. 'Shall I tuck you in?'

He lay down readily enough, but she could see that he wasn't about to close his eyes and go to sleep.

He looked at Matt. 'Did you find the little boy?'

'We did. He's safe now.'

Josh seemed happy to hear that, but he lay unmoving in bed, staring straight ahead. Sasha wondered what he was thinking.

'Try to get some rest,' she said. Glancing at the cuddly toys on either side of him, she murmured, 'Look, you've two teddies to keep you company. Aren't you a lucky boy?' So Matt had managed to retrieve the one that Jane had taken away. That was good. She smiled, wrapping the quilt around his shoulders.

'I want Mummy,' Josh said, sticking his thumb in his mouth. 'Will you find my mummy?'

Sasha didn't know what to say. It was heartbreaking, hearing the child say it aloud. What could she do?

Matt came and crouched down by Josh's side. 'We'll keep on looking for her,' he said. 'I promise.'

Josh's eyes were still wide open. 'You'll bring her home?'

'I'll do my best.'

Josh's mouth was straight. He must have been hoping that Matt could give him a better answer than that. Sasha could almost feel Matt's pain as though it were her own.

She said quietly, 'Tell me about your mummy, Josh. What makes her happy, do you know? Can you remember anything that she likes…things she likes to do, places she likes to go?'

Josh was thoughtful. 'She likes my pictures.'

She nodded. 'I'm sure she does. You draw lovely pictures.' Sasha was silent for a moment, and then said, 'Do you look at other pictures with your mummy sometimes? Perhaps you look at photos. Have you done that?'

He nodded solemnly and then gave a wide yawn. He was fighting sleep. Things were on his mind, though, and he wasn't about to close his eyes and give in.

'Were any of the photos special ones? Ones that you and Mummy liked best of all?'

'We went seaside,' he said, his voice fading. 'I played on some rocks and Mummy said, "You be careful."' He yawned again. 'She was laughing 'cos I splashed her. I splashed her a lot.'

'That was funny, wasn't it?'

He nodded sleepily. 'She had to dry herself in the cabin.'

'Were you and Mummy there on your own?'

'Me and Mummy,' he said, his voice drowsy. His mouth crooked a little at the corners, and his eyelids started to close. 'Me and Mummy,' he said, and this time it was a breathy little sigh.

Sasha sat with him for a little longer. Matt stayed by her side, looking at the sleeping child, and after a while he said in a low voice, 'I think we can leave him now.'

She got to her feet carefully so as not to disturb the boy, and quietly left the room. Matt followed, pulling the door closed behind them.

Downstairs, in the living room, he said, 'I think I know the place he was talking about. They were only there for a weekend, and it was a long time ago. I'm surprised he remembered it.'

'It must have been special, then…perhaps it was

special for both of them. Do you think Helen could have gone back there?'

'She might have.' Matt looked at his father. 'Do you remember the cabin where Helen stayed a couple of years ago?'

William pulled in a quick breath and nodded. 'I do. I'd forgotten it completely, but now I recall that at the time she said it was quiet and peaceful and she wished she could have stayed there for longer.'

'We hadn't thought of it, had we? We concentrated on places where she'd stayed for a week or more.' Matt looked at his watch. 'It's about an hour's drive from here. I think I'll go and check it out.'

'It's very late,' William said. 'Are you sure you want to do it right now? You've had a long day, with one thing and another.'

'I know, but I don't want to wait. Josh is relying on me to find his mother, and if she is there, she's more likely to be in the cabin at night. In the daytime she could be out walking somewhere, and I might never find her.' He made to move away, but his father stopped him.

'Stay for a few more minutes and have a cup of tea and something to eat. You'll think more clearly when you've some sustenance inside you.' He turned to Sasha. 'You too, love. Sit yourself down on the settee and help yourself to a sandwich.'

'Thanks,' Sasha said. She sat down as he'd suggested and saw that he had set food out on a low coffee-table. She hadn't realised how hungry she was, or how much the night air had chilled her. Now, as she drank tea and bit into soft bread and tangy cheese, she began to feel better.

She glanced at Matt. 'I want to go with you,' she said. 'If your sister is there, and she's unwell, you might need some help.'

He looked at her, and she half expected an argument. He opened his mouth as though he was going to say something and then changed his mind. He said, 'Thanks. You're probably right, and if it hadn't been for you, I would never have thought to look there.'

She smiled. 'I'll ring Sam and let him know what's happening.'

William was still mulling over the discovery of the cabin. He looked at Matt and said, 'Come to think of it, you must have blocked it out of your mind. It was where you stayed for a while, wasn't it…when you were making up your mind what to do about the offer of a specialist post? That's how Helen came to know about it. I remember your girlfriend—Natalie— wasn't very happy about things at the time, was she? She didn't want you to leave. She wanted you to stay on at the hospital with her, but in the end you decided to take the job.'

Matt grimaced. He didn't answer his father, and William began to look uncomfortable, as though he realised he'd said too much. Sasha tried to pretend that she hadn't been paying attention, but it was fairly clear that Matt had left the girl behind despite her pleas.

Perhaps Nathan had been right when he'd said that Matt didn't stay around to pick up the pieces. His career was important to him—more so than his relationships from the sound of things.

Matt finished his tea and then stood up and started to gather things together in his backpack. 'If Helen is there, I'm not sure what to expect. Before she left, she was having restless nights and bad dreams and headaches, and she was showing all the signs of anxiety. By now she could be very stressed out, and possibly irrational. I think we need to be prepared.'

'What do you want me to do?' Sasha asked. 'Is there anything I should take with me?'

He shook his head. 'Just be there. That will be enough. She might be glad of having a woman to talk to.'

'You should perhaps put some extra blankets in the car, just in case,' William said. 'She might be shocked or cold. I'll go and fetch some from upstairs.'

He hurried away, and Sasha sent Matt a quick glance. He was grim-faced and she guessed he was thinking about his sister. Nothing else mattered to him right now but the possibility of getting her back.

They went in Matt's car, and Sasha leaned back against the upholstered seat and tried to keep her mind on the task in hand. Matt's hands were firm on the wheel, steady and confident, though he was driving at a fast pace, as much as the speed limit would allow. He took the bends with ease, and his concentration was fixed on the road ahead.

The intimacy of the situation crowded in on Sasha. She couldn't help but be conscious of his every movement, of the strength of his thighs as the muscles bunched when he changed gear or accelerated, of the way his hands gripped the steering-wheel, of his nearness to her.

She had been close to him all evening, closer than she had ever dreamed she might be, and yet she wanted more, so much more. She had never felt this way before about any man. What on earth was the matter with her?

After almost an hour on the road, Matt turned the car off the country lane they had been travelling along and steered it onto what looked like a dirt track away from the main road. He cut the engine.

Sasha peered out into the darkness. From the silver light of the moon she could just about make out the outline of a cottage, or maybe a cabin. 'Are we here?' she said.

'Yes, this is the place. The cabin is set back a little from the road. It overlooks the sea, though, of course, you can't see that at this time of night.'

She could hear the sea, though, as she climbed out of the car and the sound of the waves crashing onto the shore met her. Involuntarily, she shivered, and immediately, Matt's arms went around her. 'Are you cold? Let me warm you.'

'I'm all right,' she managed. 'It's just so isolated out here.' The wind rustled through the trees and the branches moved eerily against the skyline.

He held her close. 'I knew I shouldn't have brought you out here. You've had enough for one day. I'm sorry. I should have listened to my better judgement.'

'No. I wanted to be here with you. This isn't something you should do alone.' Suddenly, as he hugged her to him, she knew that she would never be afraid while he was with her.

His face was in shadow, but she sensed that he was smiling down at her. 'You're a wonderful woman, do you know that? No matter what the cost, you seem to want to help out. What am I going to do with you?'

'I've no idea.' The truth was, she wanted to be with him. She wanted to spend every moment she could being near to him.

He chuckled, and bent his head to her, and in the next moment he was kissing her soundly, so thoroughly that it took her breath away. She wanted the kiss to go on and on. It felt so right, so good, and she could have stayed locked in his arms for all time.

A sensation of heat enveloped her. She loved the feel of him so close to her, the warm sensation of being protected by strong arms, as though nothing could ever hurt her again.

'Thank you for being here,' he muttered against her lips. 'You're very sweet. You know, I could get used to having you around.'

His words fanned the embers of hope and brought a little glow to life in her. She felt the same way. It was good to have him near, to be held as though she was special to him.

She smiled up at him. 'I want to do what I can. I've been so worried about little Josh. I'll be really happy if we manage to find your sister.'

'Me, too. Thank you for talking to Josh and making me remember the cabin. I don't think it would ever have occurred to me. At least it's one more place to try. I'd forgotten all about it.'

It was true, wasn't it? She had drawn out the one possibility that they had overlooked. What was it his father had said? Matt had blocked the memory of the cabin from his mind. Why was that…was it really because of the woman he'd left behind when he'd made the decision to pursue his career?

And now Sasha was falling for him and even daring to think of a future that might include him. Wasn't that a foolhardy thing to do, given how he'd behaved before? Was she mad? Had she completely lost her senses? Wasn't the same thing going to happen to her, in time?

Matt would want her for a while, and then he would move on. He had done it before, and who was to say that he wouldn't do it again? Why would she put herself in a situation that could only lead to heart-ache? Hadn't she had enough let-downs in her life already?

CHAPTER SEVEN

MATT led the way along the gravel path towards the front of the cabin, and Sasha followed, her steps cautious in the dark.

'I think we should make our way round to the back,' he said. 'We'll look to see if there's a way we can get in. There might be a window that has been left open somewhere.'

'What if your sister isn't the one who's renting the place?' Sasha was worried that they might be intruding on someone's privacy. The cabin was in darkness, but that could simply mean that the occupier was asleep in bed. 'If you break in you could frighten whoever's living here, not to mention that it would be a criminal act.'

'We'll knock first, but if there's no answer, I don't see that we have a choice. There's no car here to give us a clue. Helen left hers behind, and I'm guessing that's because she didn't want to be spotted driving it. She must know that we would contact the police when she went missing. That's probably why she hasn't used her bank card either. She doesn't want to be traced.'

He made a face. 'She could try to stay quiet and hide, and pretend that she isn't here, but I'm not giving up now that I've come this far.'

He rapped on the front door, and when no one came to see who was there, he went around the back and did the same thing. There was still no response from inside the cabin.

He called out, 'Helen, are you there? Helen, it's Matt. Will you open the door for me?'

No one answered, but there was a soft thud from inside the cabin. 'I thought I heard something,' Sasha whispered.

'So did I…as though someone is moving about inside the house.' He called his sister's name. 'Helen… it's Matt. Are you there?'

There was silence now, and Matt tried again. 'Helen, I've come to help you. Will you talk to me? Please, open the door.'

There was still no answer, and he called out, 'I'm not going to go away. I'll stay here all night if I have to. Talk to me, Helen, please.'

A light went on inside the cabin, and Sasha sucked in a breath. Perhaps whoever was inside would at least make themselves known to them.

A moment later, she heard the sound of a bolt being drawn back, and then the door was slowly pulled open. A young woman looked out. Her long brown hair was tousled and she was wearing a crumpled cotton top and jeans that hung on her as though she had lost weight. Her grey eyes were wide and frightened, and she clutched at her chest as though she was in pain. Her brow was knotted, and her gaze was distracted.

'Helen…' Matt moved forward and took the girl in

his arms, hugging her to him. 'You don't know how glad I am that I've found you. I've been so worried about you.' He looked at her, taking in her stricken expression, the way her slender body shook. 'You're safe now,' he said. 'I'm not going to let anyone hurt you. I'm here to help you.'

The door opened up into a large room, with a settee to one side and an armchair facing a huge brick fireplace. There was no fire lit, and the room seemed cold and cheerless.

Sasha followed them in and shut the door behind her. Helen looked at her, and the fear in her eyes was plain to see.

Matt said quietly, 'This is a friend of mine. Her name's Sasha. She's a doctor, and she works with me in A and E. She came with me because she wanted to help. She's not a threat to you, I promise.'

Sasha smiled at the girl. 'It's cold in here,' she said. 'Shall I see if I can get a fire going?' She glanced at the hearth. 'There are some logs I can use, and I'll find some paper to get it started.'

Helen didn't answer, and Sasha looked around once more and saw that there was a small kitchen to one side. She said, 'As soon as I've done that, I'll see about making us something to drink.' With any luck, there would at least be milk in the fridge and the makings of a cup of tea.

Helen gripped Matt's jacket and spoke for the first time. Her eyes were frantic. 'How is Josh?' The words came out as a cracked whisper.

'Josh is fine, but he misses you. He asks for you every day.'

Helen was white-faced, stricken. 'I'm no good for him.' She shook her head. 'He needs someone strong.'

'He needs you.'

Sasha busied herself with lighting the fire, leaving Matt to talk to his sister. It seemed best to do that. The girl was clearly anxious, and it was fairly certain that she had been neglecting herself. Sasha doubted that she had slept properly in weeks.

Sasha heard her say that her chest felt tight, and that her head was hurting, and when Sasha brought in a tray of tea just a few minutes later, Matt handed Helen a tablet that he had taken from his medical bag, and helped her with her cup.

'This should take the pain away,' he said, 'and I'm going to give you something to relieve the anxiety. When you're feeling a little bit calmer, we'll talk some more.'

When he was sure that his sister had swallowed the medication and was no longer as agitated as before, he helped her to lie down on the settee, and Sasha went to find a blanket to cover her. The room was gradually beginning to warm up, and once she knew that they weren't going to whisk her away and send her to some strange hospital, Helen seemed more inclined to rest her head on the cushions and accept their help.

She closed her eyes and drifted into a doze. Matt took Sasha to one side and said quietly, 'I think she'll sleep for a while. I'm going to drive to a late-night garage and see if I can pick up some provisions. There's nothing in the kitchen cupboards except for milk and tea. At least we can try to get some food inside her, and then we might start making some headway. I'll be as quick as I can.'

'Do you want me to go instead?'

He shook his head. 'I know the area. I know where the nearest garage is.'

That was true enough. He had stayed here before, hadn't he? 'What do I do if she wakes up and tries to run away again?' she said in a low voice. 'I might not be able to stop her.'

'Phone me. I'll start straight back. She won't get far on foot.'

She saw him out and then went and sat beside Helen, watching the girl as she slept. It was distressing to see her looking so fragile. What had driven her to this state, where she would leave the child she loved and neglect herself to the point where she was beginning to look emaciated?

After around half an hour Helen's eyelids flickered. Perhaps she had heard a log crackle in the fire or the sound of a car in the distance, but whatever it was that had disturbed her, she slowly opened her eyes and looked around. Her glance was fearful, guarded, and she said huskily, 'Where's my brother?'

'He's gone to get some food—bread and butter, the basics really. He won't be long.'

Sasha began to worry that Helen would take it into her head to leave. Surely Matt would be back soon?

Helen tried to sit up. She stared around her and said in a cracked voice, 'Matt always knows what to do. He has everything worked out.'

'He's only gone to get food,' Sasha said, concerned that Helen would read more into his absence. 'He thought you hadn't been eating properly and it's making you ill. He cares about you, and he wants to see you get better.'

'I don't deserve anyone's help,' Helen whispered. 'I can't do anything right.'

'Of course you can. You have a lovely little boy, and that's the best thing you could ever do, to bring him into the world. He needs you.'

Helen looked at her, her eyes large, questioning. 'Have you seen him?'

Sasha nodded. 'I saw him today, at his grandad's house. He couldn't sleep. He had his teddy next to him, but he still couldn't settle. He kept asking for you.'

'Did he have his cot blanket?'

Sasha frowned. 'No, I don't think so. He was in a bed. He had a duvet.'

'No…he never goes to sleep without his blanket to cuddle. He's always had it, since he was a baby.'

'I'm sorry.' Sasha was afraid that the girl was becoming agitated again. 'I didn't know. Perhaps Matt will know where it is. You see, you're his mother; and only you know all the things that make Josh happy. We can only do so much. It's you he needs.'

Helen shook her head. 'Adam said I was useless.'

'Adam?' Sasha's brows met. 'Is that your ex-husband?'

'He said I couldn't do anything right.'

'What does he know about anything? He didn't stay and look after Josh, did he? He left you to do that on your own. I don't think you should take any notice of a man who couldn't stay and support his wife and child.'

'I'll never be any good at anything. I'm the odd one out.' Helen was silent for a while, deep in thought. Then she said, 'My dad's a clever man. He's a doctor, and my mum was a nurse, a midwife. She died just as I was leaving school. Everything went wrong after that.' Helen's mouth was sad, and Sasha guessed she was remembering the past.

'That must have been awful for you. I'm so sorry.' She went on quietly, 'Your father and your brother think the world of you, you know. They've both been beside themselves with worry about you.'

Helen gazed at her. 'You work with Matt, don't you? I can never be like him. He does well at everything. He studied hard and he passed all his exams and then he went on to become a doctor. It was what he always wanted to do, but he didn't even stop then. He took more exams, and he specialised in air-sea rescue and even that wasn't enough for him. He made up his mind to be a consultant. I don't suppose he'll stop there. There will always be better and bigger things to try.'

'Does that bother you?' It worried Sasha, to think

that he might be moving on, but she wasn't about to confide that to his sister.

Helen stared at her, but her eyes were bleak. 'In a way.' Her voice broke. 'I'll never live up to the rest of my family.'

'You don't have to.' Sasha reached forward and held her hand. 'They love you as you are, and as for little Josh, he couldn't care less whether you're good at anything. He just wants you to be his mother and that's the best job in the world. He wants you to cuddle him and read him stories and tuck him up in bed at night. You don't have to prove anything to anyone.'

The cabin door opened and Matt came in. When he saw that Helen was awake, he gave Sasha a quick glance as though to ask if all was well, and she nodded imperceptibly. He was laden with packages, and he elbowed the door shut and came towards them, giving his sister a quick smile.

'How are you feeling? Is the head any better? And the pain in your chest?'

Helen swallowed hard. 'They're both much better,' she said huskily. 'Thanks.'

'That's good.' He put down the grocery bags on a table and went over to his sister. 'I'll make us some food,' he said. 'How about some soup and crusty bread? Could you manage that?'

Helen looked away. 'I don't know. I haven't felt like eating lately.'

'Well, we'll have to put that right. I'm going to put these groceries away, and then we'll see how you feel.' He sat down beside her, giving her a hug. He spoke to her quietly, and Sasha discreetly moved away and started to take the provisions into the kitchen.

He was still talking to Helen some minutes later, so she heated the soup and put crusty bread onto plates. Then she set out a bowl on a tray, filling it with the nourishing broth and carried it through to the living room. It smelt appetisingly of vegetables and she hoped that Helen would at least try a little.

She did. Matt coaxed her, and between them they managed to get enough food into her to bring some colour back to her cheeks.

After a while, Matt said, 'I think you should try to get some sleep now, and in the morning I'll take you to see Josh. Would you like to do that?'

Helen nodded. 'I didn't mean to hurt him.' She looked up at him anxiously. 'Do you think he'll forgive me?'

'He'll be overjoyed to see you. I'll tell him that you were poorly, and that's why you weren't able to be with him—that way it will be easier for him to understand. Once you're back with him, we'll get you some help…a live-in nanny, perhaps, to make things easier for you until you can manage alone, and some counselling sessions to help sort out where things went wrong. Perhaps you and Josh should stay at Dad's house for a while. Dad will be glad of the company, and Josh is used to being there now.'

He looked at her intently. 'Will you go along with that, Helen? I don't want to push you into anything, but I want to help you to see that you can do this. We're all here for you.'

'I can't do it on my own.' She looked at him, a panicky expression in her eyes.

'You're not going to be on your own. I'll see you every day, and so will Dad. We won't leave you, I promise.'

Helen nodded. 'I'll do what I can. I want to be there for Josh. It's just that I don't know if I can do it. I'm scared. I'm afraid of getting it wrong.'

Sasha put her arm around her. 'You're bound to feel that way for a while, but we won't let you struggle on your own. If ever you need someone to talk to, you can give me a call and I'll come over to be with you. Promise me that you'll do that?'

'I will. Thanks.'

Sasha helped Helen to lie back down on the settee. There seemed to be little point in moving her to a cold bedroom—at least here there was the warmth of the fire. She tucked the blanket around her and dimmed the light.

Helen began to doze. Matt said, 'I'm going to stay here with her, just in case there are any problems in the night. I think we should both try to get some rest. We still have a full day's work to do tomorrow.' He glanced around the room. 'I'll curl up in the armchair. Do you want to use the bed? There are extra blankets in the cupboard. I know it isn't going to be as warm in there, but at least you should be more comfortable.'

'Thanks. Yes, I'm exhausted.' She sent him a quick look. 'Do you think she's going to be all right? I mean, with the counselling and so on. Will it be enough?'

'I'll make sure she has some anti-anxiety drugs to tide her over this bad patch. Talking to her has made me realise just how bad things were with her and Adam. He made her feel totally worthless. There's a lot she didn't tell me before, but now that it's out in the open at last, I think she'll have a good chance of making a recovery.'

'I'm glad of that.' Sasha was relieved. 'I thought you were really good with her...very patient, and ready to listen. It's what she needed.' He had been so strong and caring, so dependable, that it brought a lump to her throat.

'My dad will help out, too. I rang him and told him what was happening. He was really pleased that we had found her. He suggested that she and Josh go to live with him.'

'I can imagine his reaction. He must have been so concerned about what was happening.' She hesitated, then said cautiously, 'You mentioned getting a nanny...'

'And that worries you?' Matt cut in. He made a wry face. 'Do you want to do the choosing this time?' He looked at her expectantly. 'I know it's a lot to ask, but you might be more successful at it than me. Perhaps a woman's instinct is what's needed.'

Her eyes widened. She was amazed that he trusted her with such a task, but she wasn't going to turn him down, given what had happened last time. The burn on Josh's chest had cleared up nicely, but that was no thanks to Jane.

'Yes, I'll do it…with Helen's input, too. I feel as though I've formed a bond with her. We've only just met, but I like Helen. It makes me sad that she's suffered so much.'

It had been an eye-opener, too, talking to her about her brother. She had guessed that Matt was ambitious, and it was common knowledge at the hospital that he was constantly striving to add to his capabilities. Was he going to be satisfied to stay in his present job? It seemed unlikely. Wouldn't he want to move on to bigger and better things, as Helen had said?

The thought sent a chill through her. She shouldn't get to care for him too much, should she? But wasn't it already too late?

In the morning, they were up and about early, quickly gathering together Helen's few belongings. Helen was nervous, apprehensive about seeing Josh, but Sasha could see that she was excited, too.

When they got back, Matt's father ushered them through his front door and into the living room, where Josh was playing with his toys on the carpet. 'I haven't told Josh anything,' William said in an aside to his son, 'just in case things should go wrong.'

Matt nodded. 'I think that was a wise decision.' He turned, and brought Helen into the room.

Josh was busy racing his cars along a track, and didn't look up. Helen watched him, her eyes large, drinking in the sight of him. A look of panic came into her eyes, and she half turned, ready to go back towards the door, when Josh suddenly glanced up.

'Mummy…Mummy,' he cried, scrambling to his feet. He came and flung his arms around her knees, holding onto her as though he would never let go.

Helen hugged him, and Sasha could see that the girl was overcome with love for Josh. She breathed a silent sigh of relief. Things were going to be all right.

They stayed to have breakfast at William's house, and afterwards he said, 'They'll be fine with me. You two get yourselves ready to go off to work. I'll take care of Helen and Josh. I'll clear away the breakfast dishes, and then we'll go out into the garden. Helen always felt good out there, and Josh can play on his bike.'

Sasha went into the living room to retrieve her bag. Matt came in a moment or so later, and said, 'You've been so good with Helen. I can't tell you enough how thankful I am to you for giving me the idea of where I could find her. Josh is thrilled to bits to have her back.'

'It's wonderful to watch him with her, isn't it?' Sasha's eyes were bright as she looked at him.

He moved towards her. 'It is. And it's been wonderful having you here with me over these last few hours. I knew it was going to be difficult, fetching her back, but having you with me made it so much easier.' His hands slid around her waist and he tugged her towards him. 'You can't know just how much I have wanted to do this…'

His head lowered, and he kissed her, drawing her

up close against him so that her soft curves were crushed against his hard masculine frame. The kiss was possessive and passionate, drawing the breath from her body, making the blood rampage through her veins like fire. She returned the kiss in full measure, heady with sudden desire, needing him, wanting him with every fibre of her being.

Her hand lifted to cup his face, and then slid around to the nape of his neck and tangled in the crisp line of his hair. He was strong and capable, protective, everything she wanted in a man. Her lips softened against his, trembling with longing, desperate for his touch.

He rained kisses on her face, her throat and lower, nudging aside the unbuttoned edge of her cotton top. His lips were warm on the curve of her breast, and she melted against him, wanting to be one with him.

Then the door clattered open, and they broke apart. Sasha's body quivered with the shock of wrenching away from him.

'What you doin'? Are you going to work?' Josh stood and stared at them, and then, losing interest, said, 'I want my truck. I want to show Mummy my truck.'

Matt said evenly, 'You mean the red one?' He bent down, retrieved the truck from the floor and passed it to Josh. Sasha was amazed that his hand was so steady. She was still shaking inside, reeling from the abrupt end to the kiss.

Josh inspected the truck and seemed happy with it. Sasha ran a hand through her hair, and said, 'I'm off to work now, Josh. I'll see you again, soon, I expect. Have a good day with your mummy and your grandad.'

She didn't stop and look back at Matt. She daren't. Perhaps it was just as well that Josh had interrupted them. It was crazy to think that anything could come of a relationship with Matt, but her mind seemed to be taking a holiday at the moment and her heart was doing all of the running.

At the hospital she made a quick phone call to check on her mother's progress. The news wasn't good, and it troubled her, but she had only just arrived on time for her shift and she couldn't get away right then. She arranged to go and visit later that day, and now she busied herself with her patients.

Her brother came to see her at lunchtime. 'I'm going to sit with Mum for a while,' he said. 'I'm sorry if I was short with you the other day. I've had a lot of things on my mind lately.'

'Do you want talk about it?'

Sam shook his head. 'Not really. There's nothing you can do to help out. It's something I have to sort for myself.'

'Are you sure about that?' Sasha was dismayed. This was her little brother, and for the first time in her life he was shutting her out. 'I might be able to come up with something, if only you tell me what it's all about.'

'No. I'll deal with it. As soon as I've seen how Mum's doing, I'm going to head back to university.

I've exams at the end of the week, and I need to get on top of things. I'll give you a ring when I'm there.'

Sasha wanted to talk some more, but Amanda called her away just then as a patient was being brought in, and she was needed in the treatment bay.

'Sam, you take care,' Sasha said. 'You know that I'm always here for you, if you need me.'

He nodded. As she turned to go to her patient, Sasha saw that Matt had stopped to talk to Sam. She walked with the paramedics towards the treatment bay, checking her patient as she went, and just before she disappeared into the bay she looked up and saw that Matt and Sam were still talking. They seemed to be getting on well together.

By the time she managed to get up to her mother's ward, Sam had already left.

Her mother looked pale. She was still breathless, and Sasha was worried about her.

'How are you feeling?' she asked.

'My chest is hurting,' her mother said. She struggled to get air into her lungs, and then she said, 'Sam came to see me.'

'That must have made you happy,' Sasha guessed.

Her mother nodded, but then she grimaced. 'I hope he's all right.'

'Are you worried about him?' Her mother had obviously picked up on something, and Sasha wondered if Sam had spoken to her about his problems. 'Did he say what was wrong?'

'I think he's having money troubles.' Her mother broke off, struggling to get her breath.

Sasha frowned. 'Is he? He's been working in the student bar. I thought that would give him an income.'

'It's not enough. He didn't want to take on more bank debt.' Her mother pulled on the oxygen. 'He needs more textbooks.'

'I could have helped him out, if only he'd asked.'

Her mother shook her head. 'You have enough to do, to keep us in house and home. Anyway, he said he thought it was sorted now.'

'How is it sorted?'

'I'm not sure. He said he saw Matt this morning, and he offered him a loan.' She took a few breaths. 'Did I tell you, Matt's father is coming to see me? They are such nice people.' Then she winced as pain racked her chest.

Sasha looked at her mother. She was very ill. Her condition was worsening, and something needed to be done to make her more comfortable. She made up her mind to talk to the nurse. Sam and his problems were the least of her worries right now.

'You should lie back and try to get some rest,' she said softly. 'I'm going to get the nurse to come and look at you, because your chest is really bad, isn't it? I think the doctor needs to come and see you. I'll go and get somebody now.' She stroked her mother's hand, and her mother leaned back against her pillows, too drained to answer.

Sasha slipped quietly out of the room. She was reeling from the news. Matt had given Sam a loan?

What was Sam thinking of, turning to Matt with his troubles? Why hadn't he come to her?

She felt as though she had fallen into a black hole. Ever since her father had left them all those years ago, she had taken on the role of looking after Sam and her mother. Now her whole world was turning upside down. Her mother was ill all over again, and Sam was behaving in a way that was at odds with everything she knew about him.

'I've already asked the doctor to come and see her,' the nurse said. 'He's with another patient at the moment, but as soon as he's free he's going to come and look at your mother. I do understand how worried you are, but there's no point in you waiting around. It could be some time before we can tell you anything more, and I think your mother needs to rest right now.'

'You will let me know as soon as there's any news?' Sasha asked.

'Of course. I'll give you a ring.'

Sasha said goodbye to her mother, and went back to work. On top of her worries about her mother, now she was concerned about Sam accepting money from Matt. It was so unlike him to do something like that, and she wanted to know what was going on.

She went to find Matt. She could at least ask him for an explanation.

'He's with a patient,' Megan said, 'and it's a really tricky case, touch and go whether he can pull him through. I don't think he'll want to be disturbed right now.'

When the call came from her mother's ward, the nurse told her that her mother's antibiotics were being changed yet again. 'The lab tests haven't come back yet,' she said, 'but the doctor's hopeful that this new treatment will work. I'll let you know what's happening.'

Matt was nowhere around when Sasha's shift ended, and she went home, still smarting from the news that he had given her brother a loan. It hurt that Sam had accepted help from Matt, rather than from his own sister, and it worried her that the loan might have been a sizable one.

She rang Sam's number, but he wasn't answering, and she tried again several times. Finally, late that night, she managed to get through. It wasn't Sam that answered, though.

'No, I'm just a friend of his,' a male voice said. There was so much noise in the background that Sasha found it hard to hear what he was saying. There was loud music and people talking, shrieks of laughter and the sound of bottles chinking.

'Isn't this Sam's phone?' Sasha asked.

'Yes, but he's not around. I answered it for him.'

'Is he working tonight?' Perhaps that explained the noise. If he was in the bar, he might be serving customers.

'Sorry, what's that you said?'

Sasha repeated her question.

'No, he isn't working tonight. He isn't behind the bar.'

Sasha frowned. 'Do you know where he is?'

'I saw him with a girl a while back. He was with Lucy…but now they seem to have disappeared.' The young man broke off and said something to someone else in the background. Coming back to Sasha, he said, 'Sorry, I'm going to have to go. I can't really talk above the noise of the party and it's hard to hear what you're saying. If I see Sam, I'll tell him you called.'

Sasha put down the phone and stared at it. She didn't understand what was going on. It wasn't like Sam to be partying when he had exams coming up. He had always been conscientious, determined to work hard and party when the time was right. This was completely unlike him.

She looked for Matt in A and E next day. 'He was here a few minutes ago, but he's going over to another hospital this morning,' Megan told her. 'He said something about wanting to see what the situation is with the emergency department over there. They have all sorts of fancy equipment, state-of-the-art stuff, and he wants to take a look around. He said he would be back at work tomorrow.'

That came as a shock. Why would he want to check out another hospital's A and E? 'Has he already left?'

'I'm not sure. You might catch him in the car park if you hurry.'

'Thanks, Megan.' Sasha hurried away. Her stomach felt leaden. Was he already getting ready to move on? She didn't know how she was going to face this new setback. Everything in her world was falling apart.

CHAPTER EIGHT

MATT was approaching his car when Sasha caught up with him. He was about to open his car door, and turned and looked at her in surprise.

'Hello, Sasha.' He gave her an intent stare, his dark eyes puzzled, but warm, all the same as though he was pleased to see her. 'You look as though there's something on your mind. What is it?'

Her glance flickered over him. He was wearing a dark suit that was immaculately cut, and showed off his tall, lean figure to perfection. His shirt was pristine. Was he going for an interview?

All the worries and uncertainties of the last few hours bubbled up inside her. She didn't know how she was going to stop them from fizzing over.

She said, 'I just heard that you were going off to look around another hospital. I had no idea that you were checking other places out.' Surely he would deny it, and everything would be all right once more?

He sent her a guarded look. 'Is that why you came rushing after me?' He gave a half-smile. 'I might have hoped that there would be something more…'

She stared at him. How could he stand there, playing games with her, when all the time he was planning on leaving? She said tautly, 'I don't know what you mean.'

'Have you forgotten so soon? I'm crushed.' His mouth made a crooked slant, and it infuriated her. It was all so easy for him, wasn't it? He played with fire, he stirred things up and made her want him, and then, just as the flames threatened to burn out of control, he was planning to move on without a backward glance.

She said stiffly, 'Is it true that you're going to look around another A and E department? Does it have more to offer than the one we have here?'

'I think probably it does, but I'll know more when I've seen it for myself.' He frowned. 'Why are you asking? Does it matter?'

She blinked, trying to shut out the pain of what he was saying. She ought to have known better than to expect anything different. Hadn't she learnt by now to avoid relationships? Didn't most of them end badly? Her parents had suffered and his sister's marriage had come to nothing. It hadn't even occurred to Matt that she would be hurt if he was to leave. He had been flirting with her, playing with her emotions with no thought as to how fragile they were.

She straightened her shoulders. For most of her life she had tried to be independent, to be self-sufficient, to avoid being hurt, and the one time she had let her guard down, Matt had whisked in and stolen her heart. Now he was intent on breaking it, and she couldn't let him do that. She wasn't going to let him see how much he was hurting her.

She said in a bleak tone, 'No, it doesn't matter.

Actually, I came here to ask you why you gave my brother a loan.'

He looked startled at that. 'Your brother didn't tell you that, did he?'

'No, he didn't. He would have guessed I wouldn't be very pleased about it. My mother told me.' Her gaze shifted restlessly over him. 'I don't understand what's going on… I can't imagine what you were thinking of. He could have come to me.'

'But he didn't. Perhaps you'll have to talk to him to find out why.'

'You hardly know him. Why would you want to take it on yourself to help him out? Only the other week you were asking if he was on drugs.'

He shrugged. 'Obviously, I was mistaken. When I met up with him again, I thought it would be good to get to know him, and I'm glad I took the opportunity. I like your brother. We had a bit of a chat and I found that I got on well with him. We went to the cafeteria and had lunch together—'

'And you decided to step in and sort his troubles out, just like that.' She was smarting, prickly with the thought of having her brother turn to someone else.

'It just came out that he's struggling to manage on what he earns at the bar, and it's just adding to all his other problems.'

'It didn't occur to you that he might just want to waste the money on having a good time, I suppose? You saw the state he was in when he came home from university. What was that all about? I still don't know…but you go and lend him money and the first thing he does is party all night. How do you think that makes me feel?'

His eyes narrowed. 'Are you sure that he was partying? Have you spoken to him about it?'

'I heard the party going on in the background. No, I haven't spoken to him yet. I haven't been able to contact him.'

'Well, perhaps you should do that before you start jumping to conclusions.' Matt's eyes darkened. 'I thought you had a good relationship with your brother. Was I wrong about that? You either trust him, or you don't.'

'It isn't a question of trust. This is a family matter, and he should have come to me if he was in trouble. It isn't right that you should lend him money, don't you see that?'

'No, I don't. I see no reason why I shouldn't help him out if I think it's the right thing to do. In fact, though,' he said tersely, 'I haven't lent him any money. I offered, but he turned me down.'

She stared at him, the wind going out of her sails. Sam had turned him down?

He sent her a considering look. 'Instead of rushing in to throw accusations at me, perhaps you should have taken time to think things through. I realise you've had a lot to cope with just lately, with starting a new job and your mother going into hospital, and I guess it's all been too much for you.'

He frowned. 'There's no shame in accepting help, but you can't do that, can you? Instead, you try to deal with everything yourself, and sometimes it just isn't possible. You need to be able to rely on someone else from time to time.'

Her mouth made a bitter line. How could he say that when he was planning on leaving? Who would she turn to then?

'That's easy for you to say, isn't it? You've never had to do it. You said it yourself—you're a man, and you don't need anybody. You go cutting a swathe through life, and it doesn't matter what heartache you cause, you don't stay behind to pick up the pieces, do you? You just move on, blindly following your dream. There's always something on the horizon to tempt you, isn't there?'

He looked at her steadily. 'I have absolutely no idea what you're talking about.'

'I can see that.' She pressed her lips together. 'Don't talk to me about relying on other people. I've found it doesn't work.' She ground her teeth. 'And as to this other A and E department you're intent on visiting, maybe you would do better to concentrate your efforts on fixing what's wrong with the one we have here, rather than exploring further afield.'

It rankled that all the ideas she'd put to him about changes in the department had come to nothing, and were destined for the waste bin.

'Look,' he said, his mouth twisting with impatience, 'I think you've managed somehow to wind yourself up into a state of nervous tension. I can't think how, but it's probably through lack of sleep, and no matter what I say you'll find something to argue about—I'm not going to stand here and bicker with you.' His jaw clenched. 'I have to go. I'm already late.'

He pulled open his car door and slid into the driver's seat. Sasha opened her mouth to say something, but he turned the key in the ignition and revved up the engine, and before she could get another word out he was driving away.

Things went from bad to worse after that. That afternoon, the nurse from her mother's ward called.

'I'm sorry to have to tell you this,' she said, 'but your mother's taken a turn for the worse. She's having a lot of difficulty with her breathing, but the doctor's with her and we're doing everything we can for her.'

Alarmed, Sasha said, 'What's causing the problem, do you know?'

'I'm not certain. We're sending her for another chest X-ray to confirm the diagnosis, and we'll know more then.'

'I'll come up and see her. I want to be with her.'

'That's all right. I'll talk to the doctor and tell him you're on your way.'

Her mother was still not back from X-Ray when Sasha arrived on the ward. She told herself that she shouldn't panic, that this sudden downturn was something doctors dealt with every day and took in their stride, but this was her mother, and it hurt to know that she was suffering this way.

The doctor came and spoke to her as her mother was brought back to the ward. 'The X-ray showed a pleural effusion,' he said. 'As you know, that means the underlying lung is being compressed, which is why Mrs Rushford is in pain and struggling to breathe. We're going to put in a chest drain to relieve the compression, and I'll send some of the fluid off to the lab for analysis.' He gave Sasha a reassuring smile. 'In the meantime, we'll do our best to make your mother as comfortable as possible.'

'Thank you. I know that you're doing everything you can.' She sent him a quick glance. 'Will I be able to sit with her?'

He nodded. 'In a while, just as soon as we have the drain in place. She should start to feel some relief as soon as we've done that.'

The procedure took a while but, as he had promised, Sasha was able to sit by her mother's bedside once they had finished. She held her hand and talked to her quietly, and wondered if anything else could go wrong today.

There had been no word from Sam, her mother was still dangerously ill, and Sasha had managed to alienate Matt.

More than anything, she wished that he was here with her now. She was at her lowest ebb and, despite her anxieties about him, Matt was the only one who could comfort her. She yearned for his shoulder to lean on, and she needed his strength to see her through this.

It wasn't going to happen, though, was it? He was getting ready to move out of her life, and into a new job, and hadn't she destroyed any closeness there might have been between them by ranting at him?

Her mother was still very ill the next day when Sasha went to visit her. 'It will take time for the medication to work,' the nurse said, 'but at least with the chest drain in place the compression on her lungs has eased.'

Sasha went to take a break in the cafeteria when it was time for the nurse to attend to her mother. As she was sipping at a cup of coffee, she looked up and was startled to see Helen and Josh coming through the door.

Josh ran over to her. 'I been looking for you,' he said, his face lighting up in a smile. 'Mummy said you was here.'

'Hello, Josh,' Sasha said. 'It's good to see you. Do you want to sit next to me and share my iced bun? If it's all right with your mummy?'

He nodded eagerly and sat himself down at the table, and Helen came to join them. 'Do you mind if we sit with you?' she asked.

'Of course I don't mind. I'd love to have you join me. Can I get you something to eat, and a coffee maybe?' She had no idea what they were doing here. Surely it was too soon for Helen to be around and about?

Helen shook her head. 'I'll get us something in a little while, thanks.' She gave a faint smile. 'I know what you're thinking,' she said, sitting down, 'but we're not on our own. My father is at the gift shop just across the corridor, looking for flowers for your mother. He promised her that he would visit today, and he thought it would do me good to get out of the house for a while.'

'He's probably right.' Sasha glanced at the girl. 'You certainly look better than you did when I saw you last.' Helen's hair was brushed smoothly into shape, and there was at least a faint tinge of pink in her cheeks. Her clothes were clean and neat, and she was altogether more in control of herself. 'How are things with you?'

'I feel much better than I did. I've had time to talk things over with my dad and Matt, and it's helped, really. I hadn't realised how much I'd bottled things up inside me, and it's been a relief to let it all out, to be honest. I've come to realise that I made a mistake marrying Adam. I was too young, and I was grieving for my mum, and I didn't really know him well enough. He was wrong for me.'

William came to sit with them. 'It's good to see you again, Sasha,' he said. 'You must come and visit us some time.'

'I'd like that.' She stirred her coffee absently and then took another sip. After her argument with Matt, though, it was unlikely he'd want to see her around.

William glanced at her. 'Are you all right? You look a bit down.'

'I'm fine,' Sasha said, straightening up. 'I've been worried about my mother, of course, but they are doing everything they can for her.'

'The waiting is the worst thing, isn't it?' He patted her hand in a sympathetic gesture. 'Try to keep your spirits up.'

'I will.'

She went back to work a little later, and lost herself in caring for her patients. She saw very little of Matt, and he seemed to be preoccupied with his patients. When their paths did cross briefly, he scarcely acknowledged her.

By the time her shift ended, her mother was still showing no signs of improvement and Sasha went home feeling thoroughly despondent.

She caught up with her chores and when she had finished, she looked about her. The house felt empty without her mother and Sam, and she wished more than anything that Matt was here with her. She had been so wrong to make accusations and to berate him for looking further afield.

She loved him, that was the truth of it, and she couldn't bear to see him go, but that didn't give her the right to try to stop him from doing what he wanted.

She went over to the phone and dialled his number. The least she could do was to apologise for her outburst.

He didn't answer his phone, though, and she replaced the receiver, feeling unhappy and uncertain. When her phone rang just a moment later, her heart began to pound and she stared at it, getting herself together before she dare answer it. Was it Matt who was calling?

'Hi, Sasha,' Theresa said. 'I wanted to ask how your mother is doing. Sam told me that she was still in hospital.'

Sasha pulled in a deep breath to steady her nerves and explained the situation. 'We just have to wait and hope that the antibiotics finally do the trick.'

'You must be feeling terrible,' Theresa said.

'I'm worried,' Sasha admitted. Then she asked, 'How are you? Have you started exams yet?'

'I took the first one this morning. It was hard going, but I'm hoping I've done enough to scrape through. Sam started his exams today as well.'

'How is he? I haven't heard from him for a couple of days.'

Theresa was silent for a moment, and Sasha guessed she was thinking about that. 'I've seen him looking better,' she said eventually, 'but he did come and talk to me, and I've arranged to help him with some of his revision this evening. I'm going to meet him in a little while. I'll keep you posted. I know what men are like, they never think to pick up the phone, do they?'

Theresa rang off just a minute or two later, and Sasha had only just moved away from the phone when the doorbell rang. She hurried to answer it. Was Matt out there…had he taken it into his head to come and see her? Her heart began to thump heavily in anticipation.

The doorbell rang again, and then there was a knocking on the door. It sounded urgent, and Sasha went into the hall, wondering what on earth was the matter.

Helen stood in the porch. She was alone, and Sasha stared at her for a moment. She looked edgy and restless, and her hair was dishevelled, as though she had been running a hand through it. 'You're on your own,' Sasha said. 'Where are your father and Josh?'

'Josh is asleep in bed. My father's watching him. I just wanted to go out for a while to look in on a friend who lives close by—my dad wasn't too happy about it, but I persuaded him I was going to be all right. I knew that you lived here because Matt pointed the house out to me the other day.' She was talking fast, the words tripping over themselves.

Sasha said, 'Slow down, Helen. Take your time. Come in and tell me what's wrong.' She pulled the door open wider, but Helen stayed where she was.

'The thing is, Sasha, I need your help. My friend isn't answering the door, and I know she's in there with the children. I could see them through the window. I'm sure something's wrong. I can't get my dad to come out because of Josh, and so I thought of you. Will you come with me and see if we can do something?'

'Of course. Just give me a minute. Where does your friend live?'

'Just a couple of streets away from here in a little old terraced house. She moved there after her husband left her. We're both in the same boat, and that's why I wanted to go and see her. We've both been through similar things.'

Sasha thought quickly as she slipped her arms into her jacket. Her medical bag was in her car, but she would throw in a few extra items, just in case.

'I'm ready. Let's go. You'll have to show me the way.'

She drove to the house, and parked at the roadside. 'Show me where they are,' she said.

'They're in the back of the house.' Helen dashed through the side entry that separated the house from its neighbour and unhooked the gate. 'Through here, see?'

Sasha peered in through the window. A young woman and her two children were in the room, the woman in an armchair, the children on the settee. The television was switched on, but all three of them seemed to be asleep.

She rapped on the window, hard, but they didn't wake up. 'I think you're right,' she told Helen. 'I think something's happened to them. We're going to have to get in somehow.'

'The back door's locked,' Helen said. 'I've already tried it. She was always worried about intruders, so she tends to keep it bolted at night. What do we do? There are too many small panes in the window... I don't think we can get in that way.'

'I'll break the glass in the lower panes. We might be able to lift the sash from the outside.' She turned to look at her. 'Do you have a phone on you?'

Helen nodded. 'In my bag.'

'You'd better ring for an ambulance, just in case...and then let your father know what's happening. He might be worried about you.'

Helen made the calls while Sasha searched around for something that would break the windows. She found a yard brush in an old shed and hammered the glass with it. Thankfully, the glass shattered after a few attempts, and she knocked out the rough edges and reached inside for the window catches.

The family inside were still unresponsive, and Sasha was concerned about that. What had made them unconscious? Had they taken something, or was there a problem with the gas fire that blazed warmly in the hearth?

She struggled with the catches. 'You'll cut your-self,' Helen said. 'Tie my scarf around your wrist. That might help.' She whipped a silk scarf from her bag, adding, 'Here—I've some tissues for your other wrist.'

Sasha wrapped them around her protectively and tried again. 'It's moving a little,' she said. 'Give me a hand to prise it up.'

Between them, they lifted the window, and Sasha heaved herself up. 'Be careful,' Helen said. 'Watch you don't cut your legs. There's a lot of broken glass around.'

Sasha was glad that she was wearing tough denims. Even so, she was cautious as she went through the opening. Once inside, she jumped down and hurried over to the fire, switching it off. Then she checked the woman and the two children. They were little girls, aged about five and six, and it broke her heart to see them like this, limp and unresponsive. They were still alive, though.

She went to the back door and unlocked it, letting Helen in. 'Leave the door wide open. Let's get as much fresh air in here as possible. Help me to get them out—the children first. We'll bring them out into the yard.' There wasn't a garden, just a paved area with a couple of tubs of pansies by the wall, but they could lay the family down where there was a clear space.

Helen hurried to lend a hand. Her face was pale, and she was shaking a little. 'What's wrong with them?'

'It could be carbon monoxide poisoning. There are dark smudges around the gas fire, so it could be faulty. We need to give them oxygen. I don't have enough ventilation bags for all of them, so I'll have to do mouth to mouth until help arrives.'

She was worried about how she was going to manage all three patients, but perhaps if they placed the children close together one person could operate the ventilation bags. Quickly she showed Helen what to do, and then she hurried inside the house to get the mother out.

The young woman was in a bad way, and Sasha was afraid that her condition might deteriorate fast. She dragged her outside and began to give her mouth-to-mouth resuscitation.

The children started to come around, and both of them began to vomit. 'Let them vomit freely,' Sasha said. 'I'll check their airways and we'll put them back on ventilation as soon as we can.'

She heard the sound of someone coming down the entry, and she hoped that it was a paramedic.

Whoever it was pushed at the gate, and she looked up to see Matt standing there. She sighed with relief.

'Dad told me where to find you,' he said, 'and I came straight away. What's happening? Is it carbon monoxide poisoning?' He was already kneeling beside the woman, opening his medical bag and taking out equipment.

'I believe so,' Sasha said. 'Thank heaven you're here. I think the mother will need an intravenous infusion of mannitol. Her pulse is falling, her blood pressure's rising and her breathing's irregular.'

'I'll get intravenous access. Is the ambulance on its way?'

'Yes.' She left the woman's side and went to help Helen with the girls. 'They were further away from the source,' she said. 'I think that's probably why they're beginning to rouse.'

'Will Tracy be all right?' Helen was looking anxiously at her friend.

'I hope so. Thanks to you, she'll at least have a chance. I don't like to think what might have happened if you hadn't decided to come and visit…and you had the good sense to check up on them and get help.'

An ambulance siren sounded in the near distance, and Sasha breathed a sigh of relief. The quicker they got Tracy to hospital, the better.

'I'm going to go with them to the hospital,' she told Helen. 'Perhaps you should go and let your father know what's happening. I'll phone you from the hospital to let you know how they're doing.'

'Will you? Thank you.' Helen was relieved. 'I'll not rest until I know that they're all recovering.'

'I'll drop you off at home,' Matt told his sister, and Sasha wondered if he was making sure that she would arrive safely.

'I'm so glad that you came here to help,' Sasha told him.

'Me, too.' He looked at the broken window-panes, and the glass shards by the wall. 'I seem to remember you have a way of getting yourself into difficult situations. I suppose you climbed through there, didn't you?'

She nodded. 'There wasn't any other way.'

'Did you cut yourself?'

'No, I'm fine.' He was frowning, though, and she followed his glance to her wrist. 'It's just a scratch,' she said. 'It's nothing to worry about.'

'If you say so.' He sounded dismissive, and stood up as the paramedics came along the entry. He helped them with the transfer of the patients to the ambulance, and then went to lead his sister over to his car.

The paramedics closed the ambulance doors, and it pulled away, siren blaring as it headed towards the hospital.

Matt turned to look at Sasha. 'Are you following in your car?' he asked.

'Yes.'

'I'll see you, then,' he said, and settled his sister in his car. He went round to the other side and slid into the driver's seat. He drove away without looking back.

Sasha watched the car disappear around the corner. That was it, then. It was as though he was driving out of her life, and she felt cold and empty, as bleak as a rainswept moor in winter.

CHAPTER NINE

TRACY had still not come round by the time the ambulance arrived at the hospital. As they wheeled her into the emergency room, Sasha saw that Nathan was on duty, and she was relieved about that. He was a good doctor, and she trusted him. She told him everything that had happened, and watched as the team went into action.

She was desperately concerned for this young woman, and she couldn't bear to think of those two little girls being left motherless.

'We're going to keep her on a hundred per cent oxygen,' Nathan said, 'and because she might be in danger of suffering from swelling around the brain, I'm going to give her an intravenous infusion of mannitol and dexamethasone IV.'

Sasha went to check on the children. They were beginning to come round properly, and as their level of consciousness increased, they wanted to know what was happening to their mother.

'The doctor is looking after her,' Sasha said. 'You've all been very poorly, and we're doing everything we can to make you better.'

She started back towards Tracy, and as she approached the bedside she saw that Matt was coming in through the emergency room doors. She frowned. What was he doing here?

He came over to her. 'How is she doing?' he asked.

'It's too soon to say just yet.' She glanced at him, a question in her eyes. 'I didn't expect to see you here. I thought you were staying to take care of Helen.'

'She's all right. She's with my dad. I wanted to come and see how things were going here.' He sent her a thoughtful look. 'You didn't have to come here, you know. Tracy is Helen's friend—you could have left her in the care of the emergency team.'

'I know, but I felt that I owed it to Helen to come and see how they were getting on. She's in no state to be here with them, and I know that she was worried.'

'I thought that must be it.'

Sasha pressed her lips together in an awkward movement. She said cautiously, 'About the other day…I shouldn't have spoken to you the way I did. I was out of order. It isn't up to me to question what you do.'

'You've had a lot on your mind lately. I know that you're worried about your mother, and that you're troubled about your brother. I suppose it was only to be expected that things would get on top of you.'

'Even so, I'm sorry.' She hesitated, and then asked slowly, 'How did you get on at your visit to the other hospital? Did things go well for you?'

'They went very well. It's a terrific A and E department. Everything runs very smoothly, and they have all the equipment and procedures very well organised. It must be a good place to work.'

It wasn't what she wanted to hear, but she said, 'I'm glad things turned out all right for you.'

Matt looked as though he was going to say something else, but Nathan came over to them just then and said, 'I think we're making some headway at last. It looks as though our patient is coming round. We'll have to admit her, of course, in case there are any complications, but hopefully she's on the mend.'

Sasha gave a sigh of relief. 'That's good news.' She sent Matt an oblique glance. 'I'll be able to tell Helen now. That will cheer her up.'

'Thanks, Nathan. Good work.' Matt and Sasha went over to Tracy's bedside to see for themselves, and Sasha made a last check on the children before she felt able to leave the emergency room.

'I'm going to look in on my mum before I go home,' she told Matt.

'Do you want me to come with you?' he asked. 'You might be glad of some support. I know she took a turn for the worse.'

'No, I'll manage, thanks.' If Matt was going to leave for greener fields, it would be best if she tried to get used to coping without him. He wasn't going to be around to give her any support in the near future, was he?

He frowned. 'Are you sure about that?'

She nodded. 'You've done enough for one day. I'm sure Helen needs you, back at home. She said how much it had helped to be able to talk to you and your father.'

'She seems to be making some progress, although it's early days yet. Josh is thrilled to bits to have her back with him.'

'Do you think there's any danger of her going off and leaving him again?'

'I don't think so. She loves him to bits, and I think she left because she felt useless and her self-esteem was at its lowest. Now that we've had a chance to talk to her, I think she'll be able to deal with some of the things that made her feel that way. We'll get her plenty of help, anyway.'

'I'm glad she came to me this evening. If she hadn't done that, her friend would have died, I'm sure. Give her my best when you see her, won't you?'

He nodded. They reached a turn-off point in the corridor, where he had to go one way and she had to go the other. He looked at her oddly, his expression sombre, but he made no attempt to go with her.

She said goodbye to him and went up to her mother's ward. It was an incredibly lonely feeling to be so close to him and yet so far apart.

'Your mother seems to be resting more peacefully,' the nurse on duty told her. 'I think the antibiotics are beginning to do their work now, and it's possible that we might be able to take out the chest drain tomorrow.'

'That's wonderful news,' Sasha said with a smile. 'Is it all right if I go and see her? I know it's late.'

'You can have just a few minutes with her. She

really needs to get as much rest as possible. Try not to disturb her too much.'

Sasha went and sat with her mother for a while. They didn't say a lot because her mother was sleepy, but it was clear that Ellen was happy to see her, and Sasha was relieved that she was making progress at last.

'I'll come in and see you again tomorrow,' she said after a few minutes. 'I'll bring you some magazines…you might feel more up to reading them when you feel a little better in yourself.'

Her mother nodded. 'I expect I will. I'll look forward to tomorrow.'

Sasha drove home. The house was empty and unwelcoming, and she switched on the lights and went into the kitchen to make herself a hot drink. She ought to be feeling good about things now that her mother was showing signs of getting better, but she couldn't rid herself of the thought that Matt was going away. It was a bleak thought, and the future stretched before her like a void.

She stared out of the kitchen window into the darkness beyond, and then the doorbell sounded, and she drew herself up with a start. Who could that be? Not Helen, surely?

'Hello again,' Matt said. 'May I come in?'

She pulled the door open, and waved him in, uncertain as why he was there, but her heart was already racing in response. He was wearing casual clothes, chinos and a shirt that was open at the throat. He looked good, and she wanted to weep.

'I've just made a pot of tea,' she said, getting herself together. 'I'll bring a tray through to the living room. Is everything all right? Is there a problem with Helen?'

'Things are fine,' he said. 'Helen's over the moon that her friend and the children are on the mend.'

'I'm glad.' Sasha brought a tray into the living room and set it down on the coffee-table. She had no idea why he was there, or what was on his mind. 'Sit down,' she said, waving a hand towards the sofa.

The phone rang and she stared at it resentfully. She didn't want any interruptions right now. She just wanted Matt.

'Aren't you going to answer that?' Matt asked.

She nodded, and walked over to the bureau and picked up the receiver. Sam's voice came to her from the other end of the line.

'I just wanted to know how Mum was doing,' he said. 'Theresa told me that she had a setback—is she any better now?'

'She's much more comfortable now,' Sasha told him. 'I've just been to see her, and the nurse is hopeful that she's going to make a good recovery.'

'Thank heaven for that. I was worried about her.'

That sounded much more like the Sam Sasha knew. She said, 'How are things with you? Did you cope all right with the exams?'

'They weren't too bad. Better than I expected, anyway.'

'That's good.' She glanced at Matt and he mouthed

Sam's name with a questioning lift of his brow. She nodded to him.

Sam paused, as though he was thinking things through, and then he went on, 'Theresa told me that you were worried about me. You didn't need to be.'

'That's easy for you to say. When I rang you and heard the party going on in the background, I must admit I was a little concerned. I didn't think it was like you to be partying when you had exams coming up.' She saw that Matt was helping himself to tea.

'It was a friend's twenty-first birthday celebration. It was bad timing, but I'd made up my mind to leave early—only I've been having trouble with this girl, Lucy. She's a bit of a wild thing, and she likes to drink, and I've been trying to do what I can to get her back on the straight and narrow. It's meant a lot of late nights, trying to sort her out, and that's why I've been so exhausted lately.'

Sasha pulled in a breath. 'I knew there had to be a reason. What's happened about it? Did you manage to sort things out?'

'In a way. Theresa told me I was wasting my time, but I didn't really want to give up on her. In the end, Theresa suggested that I take her to the welfare office and explain the problem to them. They were great. They said that they would do what they could for her, and they managed to get Lucy to sit down and talk to them.'

Sasha frowned. No wonder he had been in a state. It was much more like Sam to do what he could for someone than to cast aside his cares. She ought never to have doubted him. 'That must have been really difficult for you. I didn't realise what you were going through—why on earth didn't you tell me?'

'I didn't want to worry you. I knew you had enough on your plate with making sure that Mum was all right, and with your job and everything. To be honest, I'm glad that I was able to pass Lucy over to the welfare people. These exams are really important to me.'

'I'm glad things have worked out for you. What about your job at the bar, though? Isn't that too much for you?' Sasha was still worried about what he had said to her mother about being short of money. 'It can't be easy working, trying to earn some money and studying at the same time.'

'It's been hard, I must say, but I had a chat with your friend, Matt, the other day. He said that he would speak to the pharmacist at the hospital where you both work and see if he could get me a job in the pharmacy for the vacation. I heard from them today and it's all fixed up, so I'm really happy about that.'

She stared at Matt, her eyes widening, and he gave her a questioning look in response. To think that she had actually accused him of giving Sam a loan...she had been totally out of order. What he had arranged had been the best thing he could possibly have done, for Sam.

She spoke to Sam for a little longer, and then he hung up to go and get on with his studies. 'I'll be home at the weekend,' he promised.

Sasha replaced the receiver and glanced awkwardly.

at Matt. 'I didn't realise that you had arranged a job for Sam. That was really thoughtful of you. I don't know how I can ever thank you.'

'You don't have to,' he said. 'I've told you before that you don't have to deal with all your worries on your own.'

She grimaced. 'That's all very well at the moment,' she said, 'but you won't be around for much longer, will you? I don't see anyone else around who's going to help me.' There was no one else she wanted.

He frowned. 'What makes you think that I won't be around?'

'You're leaving, aren't you?'

'Why would I leave?'

Sasha shifted awkwardly. Was he playing games with her again? She frowned. 'To go and work at another hospital,' she said. 'That's what you do, isn't it? You move on to better things. Didn't your father say that you left a girl behind once before? You went to the cabin to think things through.'

Matt got to his feet. He made a face. 'My father had things completely wrong, but I was too concerned about Helen to go into all that at the time. The truth is, I went to the cabin because I wanted to think through my options. I could have stayed in air-sea rescue, but I had the opportunity to do something different, to be hospital-based in an A and E department. I decided that I needed to take some time to think about it.'

'And the girlfriend?' Sasha looked at him doubtfully. 'Your father seemed to think that she was upset. She didn't want you to leave.'

He shrugged. 'The girl didn't even come into it. We got on well together, but she had already found someone else, and I knew that she wasn't the one for me. The only reason she wanted me to stay was because we worked as a team.'

He moved towards her and his hands lightly circled her arms. 'There is only one woman for me. Don't you know that? I want to be with you, Sasha. I think I've known that almost from the first time I met you. I have never felt this way about anyone before.'

She looked up at him, uncertainty in her gaze. Had he really said what she thought he had said? He wanted her? 'You didn't say… I thought… I thought you would be going away. I thought your career was more important to you than anything else.'

'I want to be with you, that's the most important thing, and I doubt that you would want to move on. You have your mother to think of, and I can't see you leaving her behind. The same thing applies to me. I need to be near my sister and Josh to make sure that they're all right. I get on well with my dad, too, and I've no plans to uproot myself.'

He ran his hands along her arms in a light caress, and then he drew her close to him, his hands sliding around her waist. 'Surely, you know that I love you? I think I've known from the moment I first saw you, when you were trying to save that little boy. I thought how foolhardy you were, how reckless, and yet at the same time I thought you were so brave and determined. I never want to lose you.'

Sasha was confused. 'But why did you go to that other hospital? I thought you were going for an interview for a job.'

His brows drew together in a dark line. 'Whatever gave you that idea? I never mentioned looking for another job.' His mouth curved. 'No wonder you were so uptight with me. Does that mean that you care for me, too?'

She sucked in a deep breath. 'I didn't want you to go. I wanted you to stay with me, and then I thought how selfish I was being. I've grown so used to having you close by. I didn't understand what I was feeling, but now I know that I love you, and that scares me. I'm afraid of being lost and alone, of having it all turn to ashes.'

He shook his head. 'That's not going to happen. You have to trust me on that.' He bent his head towards her and claimed her mouth, kissing her as though he would never let her go. His hands stroked her, gently pressuring her until her soft curves melted against him.

'I need you so much,' he muttered. He kissed her mouth, and then his lips brushed along her cheek, and he kissed the lobe of her ear, and then dipped to trail kisses along the line of her throat. 'I can never get enough of you.'

She lifted her arms and wound them around his neck, kissing him with all the love and need that was pent up inside her. 'Me, too,' she murmured. 'I've been wrong about everything lately. I was so sure that you were going to leave.' Her fingers trailed over his jaw and slid down over his shoulder, tracing the line of his strong, muscled arms.

'I still don't understand why you went to that hospital,' she murmured. 'I was heartbroken when you said that it would be a good place to work.'

'I wanted see how they did things there, how they implemented changes. There's no challenge in going to work at a hospital where everything's in place and working perfectly. For me the challenge is in changing something that's not functioning too well and making it better.'

'Are you serious? You'd never any intention of going there to work?'

'It's the truth. Based on what I learnt, I've drawn up plans for making changes to our A and E department. I've been in talks with management about creating a separate paediatric wing, as you wanted. If I show them how it can be done with minimum fuss and expense, I think they will agree to it.'

'Matt…' Her voice was choked. 'I'm so proud of you. You're so caring and so thoughtful, and I should have had more faith in you.'

He looked down at her. 'I know how hard it is for you,' he said, 'but you have to put your trust in me. I won't let you down. I'll always be here for you, and you can depend on me, I promise. I love you.' He smiled. 'My family loves you.'

He brushed his thumb gently along the line of her

cheek. 'Will you marry me? Please, say that you'll marry me.'

'Oh, yes,' she whispered. 'Matt, I love you.'

He gave a relieved sigh. 'I'm glad that's settled, at least.' He looked down at her. 'Just promise me one thing…'

'What's that?'

'That you'll try to refrain from any more hazardous escapades, like exploring dangerous demolition sites and climbing through broken glass. I'd dearly like to keep you in one piece.'

Sasha smiled up at him. 'I'll do my very best,' she said, and lifted her face for his kiss.

MILLS & BOON®

Live the emotion

_Medical
romance™

0805/03b

THE ITALIAN SURGEON by *Meredith Webber*

(Jimmie's Children's Unit)

All eyes are on the newest member of the team at Jimmie's – tall, dark and handsome Italian surgeon Luca Cavaletti. Luca only has eyes for Dr Rachel Lerini. The closer Luca gets, the more she runs away – but he is determined to make her smile again – and even love again…

HER PROTECTOR IN ER by *Melanie Milburne*

(24:7)

Five unexpected deaths have brought hot-shot city detective Liam Darcy to town. Dr Keiva Truscott is first on his list of suspects. All Liam's instincts tell him she's innocent – but until the case is closed he can't possibly fall in love with his prime suspect…!

THE FLIGHT DOCTOR'S EMERGENCY
by *Laura Iding*   *(Air Rescue)*

Flight Nurse Kate Lawrence has learned through hard experience that laughter is the best healer – and it looks like Flight Doctor Ethan Weber could use a dose of it himself. The single father's lifestyle is all work and no play – something Kate is determined to change.

Don't miss out!
On sale 2nd September 2005

Available at most branches of WHSmith, Tesco, ASDA, Borders, Eason, Sainsbury's and most bookshops

Visit www.millsandboon.co.uk

FREE

4 BOOKS AND A SURPRISE GIFT!

We would like to take this opportunity to thank you for reading this Mills & Boon® book by offering you the chance to take FOUR more specially selected titles from the Medical Romance™ series absolutely FREE! We're also making this offer to introduce you to the benefits of the Reader Service™—

★ **FREE home delivery**
★ **FREE gifts and competitions**
★ **FREE monthly Newsletter**
★ **Books available before they're in the shops**
★ **Exclusive Reader Service offers**

Accepting these FREE books and gift places you under no obligation to buy; you may cancel at any time, even after receiving your free shipment. Simply complete your details below and return the entire page to the address below. You don't even need a stamp!

YES! Please send me 4 free Medical Romance books and a surprise gift. I understand that unless you hear from me, I will receive 6 superb new titles every month for just £2.75 each, postage and packing free. I am under no obligation to purchase any books and may cancel my subscription at any time. The free books and gift will be mine to keep in any case.

M5ZEE

Ms/Mrs/Miss/Mr..............................Initials ....
BLOCK CAPITALS PLEASE

Surname ....

Address ....

....

....Postcode ....

Send this whole page to:
The Reader Service, FREEPOST CN81, Croydon, CR9 3WZ